"Kathryn, don't make me wait any longer!"

Zac groaned as he broke her grip on his hands and began to run his hands over her body.

Then she reached up and wrapped her arms tightly around him, overwhelmed by the sudden joy of being able to show her love for him at last. She felt him pull her nightdress down until she was naked, and his eyes were filled with a deep hunger as he looked down at her. "We'll have a proper honeymoon right here," he said in a voice that was infinitely tender, yet exultant and triumphant.

In a few moments she felt the heat from the full length of his naked body beside her on the bed as he murmured with his mouth on her lips, "Starting now."

WELCOME
TO THE WONDERFUL WORLD
OF *Harlequin Romances*

Interesting, informative and entertaining,
each Harlequin Romance portrays an appealing
and original love story. With a varied array
of settings, we may lure you on an African safari,
to a quaint Welsh village, or an exotic Riviera
location—anywhere and everywhere that adventurous
men and women fall in love.

As publishers of Harlequin Romances, we're
extremely proud of our books. Since 1949,
Harlequin Enterprises has built its publishing
reputation on the solid base of quality and
originality. Our stories are the most popular
paperback romances sold in North America; every
month, six new titles are released and sold at
nearly every book-selling store in Canada and the
United States.

A free catalog listing all Harlequin Romances
can be yours by writing to the

HARLEQUIN READER SERVICE,
(In the U.S.) 1440 South Priest Drive, Tempe, AZ 85281
(In Canada) Stratford, Ontario, N5A 6W2

We sincerely hope you enjoy reading
this Harlequin Romance.

Yours truly,

THE PUBLISHERS
Harlequin Romances

Not the Marrying Kind

Helen Dalzell

Harlequin Books

TORONTO • NEW YORK • LONDON
AMSTERDAM • PARIS • SYDNEY • HAMBURG
STOCKHOLM • ATHENS • TOKYO • MILAN

Original hardcover edition published in 1983
by Mills & Boon Limited

ISBN 0-373-02570-X

Harlequin Romance first edition September 1983

CHAPTER ONE

KATHRYN stood and regarded the broad masculine shoulders and the back of the smooth dark head for a few moments before she spoke. 'I suppose you realise you're trespassing?' The words, when they came, were supposed to be admonitory, reproving, but the look in the laughing eyes of the man who turned to face her made it quite evident that they had no such effect.

'You surely wouldn't want to keep that magnificent view all to yourself,' he replied, amused and lazy blue eyes looking her up and down. Kathryn noticed the trace of Irish brogue at once, although she didn't need such a clue to tell her that the man was a stranger. 'It's not quite so lush and green as where I come from,' he added conversationally, at the same time turning his back on her once more, 'but it'll do.' Then, as she drew in her breath preparatory to making a biting retort, something calculated to cut him down to size, he suddenly whirled round again. 'I beg your pardon,' he said, brilliant blue eyes suddenly serious. 'I'm forgetting my manners. Allow me to introduce myself . . .'

'Please don't bother,' she interjected quickly, ignoring the outstretched hand. 'It's of absolutely no interest to me. Now, if you wouldn't mind, I'm sure you know perfectly well that this is private property and I would be glad if you would leave. That's your quickest way out.' She pointed down the broad tree-lined walk and waited, her eyes stonily fixed on his, impatient for him to be gone. At that moment Bess, her old golden Labrador bitch, appeared from the undergrowth where she had been happily rooting about and, in her usual way on seeing a stranger, sidled over to him, grinning all over her face and vigorously waving her thick bushy tail. But Kathryn sharply called her to heel and she reluctantly came and lay down at her feet, panting and smiling all over her lovely old face.

'Oh, dear,' he said softly, 'we do seem to have got off to a bad start, don't we, Miss Mallory?' At her sudden frown, he raised dark, well-marked eyebrows. 'I take it that is who you are?'

'Yes,' she answered crossly, feeling at an unexpected disadvantage. 'Who are you?'

'As you said, it's of absolutely no interest to you,' came the maddening reply, a humourless smile now hovering round his mouth, 'and since you ask so nicely, I'll be on my way. However, you might as well get used to the idea that we'll be meeting again. Perhaps you could do something about your manners in the meantime. Good day to you.'

Hands thrust nonchalantly into the pockets of his well-cut trousers, the light breeze gently ruffling the dark hair and regretfully watched by the over-friendly Bess, he strolled away from her, making no attempt to hurry, apparently completely at home in the surroundings in which he found himself, leaving her furiously watching his retreating back and with the greatest difficulty controlling an almost irrepressible urge to hurl a string of childish insults after him. His last words had incensed her to such a degree that it was all she could do to maintain a dignified silence, and wild horses would not have dragged from her the admission that there had been some justification for his remark.

Only when he had disappeared from view did she relax and walk across to where he had been standing, making a determined effort to put him out of her mind. His words about a future meeting she dismissed out of hand. She had a great deal on her mind at the moment and would not concern herself further with an insolent stranger who meant nothing to her. Instead, she raised her eyes to contemplate what had always been her favourite view of her beloved Woollerson Hall.

Rooks were cackling in the treetops, calling raucously across to one another as they went about the laborious and painstaking business of making their new nests. They were building high this year, she noticed, sign of a good summer. A solitary magpie flew down a few feet away from her, then took off again in a flash of blue-green, purple and white. One for sorrow, she counted to herself, and looked round for its mate, knowing that apart from being unlucky it was unusual to see one on its own, but she watched in vain and acknowledged that it was only too appropriate at this time, as the magpie's 'chak-chak-chak-chak' faded into the distance.

Her grandmother, who had brought her up since the untimely death of her parents in a car crash when she was two years old, had died the previous day and, although the old lady had been nearing eighty, Kathryn had not yet even begun to recover from the shock of losing her and finding herself suddenly alone. Gran had been everything to her;

father, mother, counsellor, companion and confidante, and, as she stood in her own special vantage point—so recently and flagrantly intruded upon by the dark stranger—Kathryn knew that the void which had suddenly opened up in front of her would be hard, if not impossible, to fill.

Suddenly close to tears and brought up to be scornful of such feminine weakness, she quickly focussed her clouding vision once more on the lovely spectacle before her. Woollerson Hall, which was lying so tranquilly in the early spring sunshine, had been built of Portland stone in the early part of the eighteenth century. At sunrise, the white stone would take on a yellow hue, fading to cream and then white as the sun rose higher in the sky and at sunset a blush of pink would descend on the house, turning the old Hall into a fairytale palace, a sight which never failed to thrill her.

Originally there had also been both east and west wings, but the east wing had been razed to the ground by fire some fifty years after the house had been built and, in order to redress the balance, the remaining west wing had subsequently been demolished by Capability Brown. The remaining central portion made a country seat of large but manageable proportions and had been the home of the Mallory's for many hundreds of years.

To the north and south of the house, Brown had laid out sloping lawns flanked by trees, with uninterrupted views over the surrounding Suffolk countryside. To the west were formal rose gardens, with kitchen gardens and orchard behind and beyond, now empty, was the old stable block. To the east there was a heavily wooded area which gave way nearer the house to an avenue of trees which provided shelter for visitors as they approached the Hall. The remainder of the land farther away from the house was open parkland.

And now all this was hers, Kathryn thought, a sudden lurch in the pit of her stomach reminding her abruptly and painfully that Gran was gone and she would have to shoulder the burden of the estate alone. She was the last of the Mallorys, and increasingly often of late Gran had been bluntly telling her that it was high time she found herself a husband and settled down, and Kathryn knew that it was as much for the future of Woollerson as for herself that she had been anxious, since Gran had loved Woollerson passionately and had worked tirelessly for its preservation and that of the village over which it presided. It was only natural that she should want to ensure that after her death, Kathryn—and eventually Kathryn's children—would be there to care for the family home and continue to guide its fortunes.

'I want to see my grandchildren playing at Woollerson before I die,' she had said only a few days before her death. Kathryn had looked up quickly to see whether there was anything amiss which could have prompted the remark, but her grandmother had looked her usual self, upright, autocratic, not a hair out of place on her snowy white head, piercing blue eyes fixed steadily on her granddaughter.

Kathryn winced when she remembered her answer. 'There's plenty of time,' she had said casually.

'Indeed there is not!' the old lady had retorted. 'Why can't you find some nice young man and settle down? What about young what's-his-name,

Colonel Bradley's boy? He seems a nice young chap.'

'But, Gran,' she had protested, laughing, 'you know perfectly well he's engaged to a girl he met when he was up at Oxford.'

'Only because you wouldn't have him!' her grandmother had snorted. 'You know you could have had him. Silly girl!'

Kathryn had gone to her then and put her arms round the old lady's neck and hugged her. 'But I didn't want him, darling,' she had said firmly. 'Gran, I wish you'd stop matchmaking. And in any case,' she had added, straightening, 'there's Brian.'

'Humph!' the old lady had snorted, and there had been a pregnant silence, before she rose and unhooked her stick from the back of her chair, sighing dramatically before she left the room. 'I think you know my opinion of that young man, Kathryn,' was her parting shot. 'I'm trusting to your good sense to find someone more suitable.'

Sighing deeply, Kathryn dragged herself back to the present, wondering just what it was that Gran hadn't liked about Brian. He was tall and fair, good-looking and hard-working, helping his father run the riding stables just outside the village. And she was in love with him. She had tried to imagine what life would be like married to Brian. Would he consent to live at the Hall, she wondered, and would the staff accept him as the future lord of the manor? And how would the villagers react to the idea of him as their new squire? In many respects the estate was still remarkably feudal, more than half of the cottages in the village being owned by the estate and their occupiers therefore being

Gran's tenants—her tenants, Kathryn hastily corrected herself—and it had always been of prime importance to Gran that every one of her tenants should be fairly treated, his cottage kept in good repair and any reasonable request from him seriously considered and then acted upon if it were thought to be for the good of the individual and of the village as a whole. The estate had prospered over the centuries and was now one of the richest in the county.

Undoubtedly there would be problems, Kathryn acknowledged as, calling softly to the old dog, she turned and began to walk slowly on—but then, she thought staunchly, surely there must always be some problems when two people decided to marry. Deep in thought and with Bess padding along faithfully at her side, she walked on, right down into the village, to be met on every side by sad faces and soft words of condolence. Some of the older tenants, she noticed, deeply touched, were close to tears, confirming what she already knew— that Gran had been greatly loved and respected. Which was going to make her task all the harder when she took up the reins. The standards set by the old lady were going to be difficult to live up to and she could see clearly now, as she never had before, that it was vital that she marry the right man to help her. But surely Brian was the right man, wasn't he? Everyone knew him and, so far as she was aware, liked him well enough.

She had reached the Red Lion now, the lovely old beamed inn, reputed to be the oldest hostelry in the county, with its thick thatched roof hanging in a silver-grey fringe over the leaded windows and crooked front door. In summer the landlord placed small white-painted tables and chairs outside, but it was too early in the year, yet in spite of the sunshine and any regulars who wanted to sit outside used the heavy oak benches which stayed out in all weathers, winter and summer. Although her mind was far away, Kathryn was instinctively aware that the pair of long legs sticking out across the pavement and threatening to trip her up did not belong to anyone she knew, and she realised almost in the same moment that they belonged to the dark-haired trespasser. Without quite knowing why, she paused a moment and regarded the reclining figure dozing in the sun, stretched out on one of the benches, her eyes lingering momentarily on the strong line of the jaw, the well-shaped mouth, the slightly prominent cheekbones, and the very dark hair moulded to his head in a sleek cap.

Suddenly his eyes flew open and regarded her bleakly for an instant, before he gathered in his long legs and slowly stood up, inclining his head towards her. 'Miss Mallory,' he said with a faint smile which did not reach his eyes. Then he turned on his heel and disappeared through the doorway of the Red Lion.

Kathryn's lips tightened into a straight line as she walked quickly on, and she chided herself inwardly for undoubtedly letting him get under her skin after such a brief, almost non-existent, acquaintance. There was something about him which made him hard to put out of her mind, she acknowledged, as she stalked angrily down the narrow main street. 'Damn him!' she muttered crossly under her breath. 'I wish he'd go away, whoever he is. I could certainly do without him just now!'

She was glad to see that there was no sign of him when she retraced her steps and passed the Red Lion again on her way home, and by the time she had reached the outskirts of the estate and started up the long drive, she found that she was able to forget him and concentrate her thoughts on the many problems facing her. Her main concern, she judged, would have to be the question of a replacement for Gran's agent, Mr Eliot, who was retiring in a few weeks. It was most unfortunate that his impending retirement should coincide with Gran's death, and she wondered if he could be persuaded to stay on for a little while longer. It was worth a try at any rate, she thought, as she let herself into the unusually silent house, and she resolved to approach him with the suggestion immediately after the funeral.

The next few weeks were difficult ones for Kathryn. First there was the funeral, and it was then more than ever that it was remorselessly brought home to her that she was now completely alone in the world. There was no one who had the right to sit in the front pew with her during the service, and, head held high, she walked alone behind the coffin as it was borne on the shoulders of the pallbearers on the short journey to the graveside. It was true that the entire village was there with her, many of them in tears, but Kathryn knew as, dry-eyed, she stood and said her last goodbyes to Gran, that from now on they would all be looking to her and that she would have to grow up very fast indeed if she were not to let them down.

. As the mourners left the graveside she looked round for Brian. She had spoken to him on the telephone several times since Gran died, but he had not come up to the Hall to see her and she had told herself that it must have been a misguided sense of the proprieties which had kept him away. Now she felt in urgent need of comfort, and she walked quickly over to where he was standing beside his father.

'You'll come back to the Hall, won't you?' she asked quietly. 'I would like to talk to you, Brian.'

Was she imagining things, or had he hesitated before accepting, she wondered, as she turned away to speak to Gran's solicitor, Mr Barnes? But she put the thought quickly out of her mind as she drove back to the Hall in the large black car, flanked on one side by Mr Barnes and on the other by the agent, Mr Eliot. Although neither man said very much, it was in the minds of all three of them that in a very short time they would have to meet again in order to come to terms with the new situation which confronted them. Deciding to broach the matter uppermost in her mind there and then, Kathryn turned to the agent.

'Mr Eliot, is there any chance that you could postpone your retirement and stay on for a few months?' she asked. 'I would be most grateful if you could. I'm afraid I find that I don't know as much as I should about the estate, and I'm really going to need your help.'

To her surprise, he immediately looked uncomfortable. 'Of course I shall help you all I can, Miss Kathryn,' he replied, 'but it will only be for a few weeks. My wife and I are intending to visit our daughter in Canada in just under a month. I'm afraid it's all arranged, tickets paid for and everything. We plan to stay for at least six months.

Your grandmother knew of our plans—I'm surprised she didn't mention it to you.'

'Oh, dear!' Kathryn answered, flushing in some confusion. 'Now you remind me, I believe she did. I'm so sorry, Mr Eliot, please forget I asked you. I should have remembered. I'm sure I shall manage somehow until I can find someone to take your place.' There was a sinking feeling in the pit of her stomach as she contemplated the awful prospect of coping with the hundred and one details of the management of the large estate, about which she knew precisely nothing. Too late, she remembered the countless occasions when Gran had tried to instil into her some interest in the day-to-day running of Woollerson, but she had been too busy enjoying herself, falling in love with Brian, selfishly pursuing her own ends and taking no thought for the morrow—until it was too late. With difficulty she pulled herself out of her bitter introspection as she realised that Mr Eliot had been speaking and was now apparently waiting for some response from her. 'I beg your pardon, Mr Eliot, what did you say?'

'I said, Miss Kathryn,' he answered a little reproachfully, 'that I was under the impression that your grandmother had already found someone and that it was more or less settled. Is that something else you knew nothing about?'

His last sentence was put in the form of a question but was in fact all too evidently an accusation, and, although she was tempted to make a sharp retort, she bit back the words, knowing that the rebuke was justified. 'Oh, dear,' she said instead. 'I expect Gran did mention it, but I probably wasn't listening. You see,' she turned to face him in an attempt to excuse her lack of interest, 'I never expected her to die—not so suddenly, at any rate.'

'She was nearly eighty, Miss Kathryn,' he reminded her.

'Yes, but somehow she always seemed practically indestructible,' she rejoined on a sigh. 'I thought she'd live for years longer.'

'But surely you were aware of her heart condition?'

'Yes, of course, but she always made light of it. I didn't think it was all that serious.' She was silent for a while, thinking what a bad impression she must be making on both the old men sitting in the car with her as it glided almost silently up the drive towards the house. Just before it stopped, she braced herself and spoke in what she hoped was a businesslike manner. 'I'm afraid you must both think me very selfish and foolish, but that's all changed now. I am well aware of my responsibilities and I'm determined to do my very best. When is the new agent due to arrive, do you know, Mr Eliot? And what's his name?'

The car drew up in front of the house and the black-suited chauffeur opened the door. 'I believe the name is Wilding,' the agent answered as he helped her out. 'Very well connected, I believe. I only hope he knows his job. But then,' he added hastily in case she should misunderstand him, 'I'm sure he does, or your grandmother would never have taken him on. As to when he's due to arrive, I'm afraid I have no idea. Quite soon, I would think. Then I'll have a few weeks in which to show him the ropes.'

An hour or so later, it was the turn of the solicitor, Mr Barnes. 'I'll be in touch with you in a day or so, Kathryn my dear,' he said as he took his leave. 'There's the matter of your grand-mother's will . . .'

'Yes, of course,' she said quickly. 'In a day or two.' Suddenly she found his presence suffocating, and she closed the door behind him with a sigh of relief and went slowly back into the drawing-room, which suddenly seemed enormous now that everyone had gone; indeed, the whole house seemed vast and empty now that Gran was gone, and she wandered disconsolately from room to room, looking at everything with unseeing eyes, deep in thought.

Although Brian and his father had come up to the house with the others, she had been able to have no more than a few words with him alone, and she had hoped that he would realise how much she needed him and would have stayed behind. She was beginning to get the impression that he was avoiding her, although she couldn't imagine why, unless it was because she was now the lady of the manor and had somehow, almost overnight, become unapproachable. She wondered wearily whether this was to be the pattern from now on and whether she would find everyone treating her differently. If it proved to be so, life could be going to become pretty unbearable in the very near future.

As she closed the door of the library, which was the last room into and out of which she had aimlessly wandered, she heard a bell ring in the distance and wondered who could have called on such a day. Then, with a sudden lift of her heart she thought that perhaps Brian had come back, and she walked quickly along the corridor, to be met by one of the maids. 'There's a Mr Wilding to see you, Miss Kathryn,' the girl said uncertainly. 'Shall I tell him you're not at home?'

'No,' Kathryn answered quickly, hiding her disappointment that it was not Brian after all, but glad nonetheless that the new agent had arrived so opportunely. 'I'll see him. Show him into the drawing-room.' Greatly relieved at the news of his arrival and feeling that from now on matters might be expected to take a turn for the better, she walked into the drawing-room a few moments later, a welcoming smile on her face. 'Mr Wilding, thank goodness you've come,' she said as she advanced into the room. 'No one seemed to know exactly when you would be arriving.' Then she stopped dead in her tracks and her grey eyes widened in disbelief, as the tall man standing by one of the windows slowly turned round to face her. 'You!' she gasped, and her hand which had been outstretched towards him fell to her side. 'Oh, no, I don't believe it!' She looked angrily into the brilliant blue eyes gazing steadily back at her. 'You're Mr Wilding?' Her words ended on what amounted to a plaintive wail, as she realised that in the arrogant man standing before her, the self-same dark-haired trespasser who had so riled her a few days before, she was hardly likely to find the comfort and help which she was seeking. Stupidly, as she now realised, she had somehow assumed that the new agent would be stamped in the same mould as the old one, and to imagine that the supercilious individual standing so calmly before her was even remotely like Mr Eliot in any way whatsoever was utterly laughable. He seemed perfectly at ease, she noted irritably, not in the least put out—but then why shouldn't he be? He had known all along who she was; it was she who had been in the dark.

'Zac Wilding,' he said, suddenly crossing the space between them and smiling broadly, seizing her hand in his and clasping it in a firm grip. 'You wouldn't allow me to introduce myself at our earlier meeting, if you remember.'

Kathryn took her hand away as soon as his grip slackened. 'Oh, no, it won't do, you know,' she said, shaking her head and sinking down into the nearest armchair, running her fingers distractedly through her short blonde hair. 'I thought you'd be quite different, Mr Wilding.'

'That can be a fatal mistake,' he said easily.

'What can?'

'Having a preconceived idea of what someone is going to be like. I find that one is invariably wrong. Just what sort of man had you in mind, I wonder?'

She looked at him wordlessly for a moment before answering. 'Certainly no one in the least like you,' she said slowly. 'I must admit I was hoping for someone much older whom I could rely on completely and who would be a real support to me—to begin with at any rate,' she added hastily, seeing a hint of what she guessed to be scorn in his eyes.

'I'm sure you'll find that I fit the bill perfectly adequately,' he said with a slight smile. 'Apart from not being older than I am, of course. I'm afraid I can't do anything about that.'

'How old are you?' She saw by his expression

that he did not like the question, but she felt that she had a perfect right to ask.

'Over thirty.' His reply was curt and she felt it best not to pursue the matter.

A further silence fell between them. Kathryn really had no idea what to say because, however she decided to phrase it, her next words were going to be dismissive and she had no experience in the gentle art of telling someone that they weren't wanted. As for him, he appeared to be perfectly relaxed, evidently faintly amused by his confrontation with her, awaiting her next move without any very apparent interest.

'You didn't choose a very good day to call,' she said eventually, deciding to go on to the attack, thinking that if she worked herself up to a certain pitch of acrimony it would be all the easier to tell him quite soon to go about his business. Of one thing she was very sure, and that was that she had no intention of offering him the position of agent, even if she had to carry the burden of the estate alone for some considerable time. She felt that she would never feel comfortable in the presence of this man and that it would always be an effort to be even normally polite to him. There was something about him which made her hackles rise just to look at him.

'On the contrary, Miss Mallory,' came the imperturbable response, 'I consider that I've been the very soul of tact. I've been kicking my heels down at the Red Lion, where I've been staying, for the past three days in order not to intrude until after the funeral. Naturally the landlord informed me of your grandmother's death the moment I arrived and of course I've kept a low profile in the meantime. But now it's time I got to work and, from the little I've seen of the estate so far, there's going to be plenty to do. Without wanting to be too derogatory to my predecessor, I can't help feeling that things have been allowed to get a little slack.'

'You're going much too fast, Mr Wilding,' she said icily, stung by his presumption, standing up and facing him. 'And kindly do not malign an extremely nice old man whom you've never ever met!'

'Wrong on both counts,' he said impatiently.

'What do you mean?' She felt her irritation mounting by the minute.

'One, I'm not going too fast—on the contrary, I'm not going fast enough. There's a great deal to be done. And two, I have met Mr Eliot. I made a point of tracking him down and having a brief talk with him less than an hour ago. A nice old boy, as you say, but past it.'

'Really, Mr Wilding, I can't imagine just how we've managed all this time without you!' Kathryn's voice was heavy with sarcasm and he suddenly smiled in evident amusement. 'But I repeat, you're most certainly going too fast. You seem to take it for granted that the job is yours, whereas nothing—but nothing—could be farther from the truth!' She was suddenly totally exasperated by his air of smug self-confidence and wanted spitefully to cut him down to size. But it was immediately patently obvious that she was making no headway at all. Far from being reduced to the state of confusion she had hoped for, he appeared to be enjoying himself more and more and there was a wide grin on his face as he slowly reached into an inner pocket of his jacket and drew out a letter.

'I'm afraid you're labouring under a misapprehension, Miss Mallory,' he said softly, making not the slightest effort to hide his amusement. 'The job *is* mine, and here's the letter from your grandmother to prove it. Won't you read it?' He pressed the single sheet of paper into her unwilling hand and most reluctantly she unfolded it and quicky scanned its contents. It was a formal letter from her grandmother briefly confirming his appointment as the new agent for the estate with effect from the date two days hence.

'But of course you must realise that my grandmother's death has altered the situation,' she said with a composure she was far from feeling. 'Surely you can see that. And therefore . . .' she paused and fixed him with a stony stare, 'this is worthless.' And with her eyes still coldly fixed on his, she slowly and very deliberately tore the letter into four pieces and, crossing the room, dropped them into the wastepaper basket. When she turned and looked at him once more, she was pleased and just a little frightened to see that the smile had been wiped off his face, and for a long triumphant moment she was aware that he was making a visible effort to control his emotions.

'Your extremely childish action will get you precisely nowhere, Miss Mallory,' he said quietly after a few moments. He took a step towards her and she took an involuntary step backwards. She saw a muscle twitch at the corner of his mouth and she was suddenly acutely aware that she knew absolutely nothing about the man. She thought very briefly that he was going to attack her and reached behind her to grope for the bellpull to summon help, but he was too quick for her, and she gasped as her wrist was seized in a strong and painful grip. 'Do you really want to make an even bigger fool of yourself than you have already?' he asked, the brogue in his voice suddenly very strong. She saw the quick flash of anger in his eyes before he pushed her roughly down into a chair and moved a few paces away from her. 'Now, let's have done with this infantile behaviour and talk some sense, shall we?' It was clear that he had himself well in hand now. 'In spite of your actual words and your only too obvious dislike of myself, there remains one fact which makes a nonsense of everything you've said and reduces your attitude to mere prejudice.'

'And that is?' Kathryn asked stonily as she sat rubbing her wrist.

'The fact that you were obviously glad to see me—until you saw my face.' He waited for her answer, but, receiving none, continued, at the same time walking across the room and staring out of one of the windows, 'It therefore occurs to me that you find yourself in something of a fix. Your Mr Eliot, as I've just discovered, is about to take himself off for a prolonged holiday in Canada, leaving you to cope alone. He has told me that you know absolutely nothing about the running of the estate, and from my own observation on an admittedly short acquaintance, I have the distinct impression that you know precious little about anything at all—apart from a talent for enjoying yourself and avoiding your responsibilities. Kindly let me finish.' While he had been talking he had kept his back towards her, yet he evidently judged with deadly accuracy the turmoil of hostility which was consuming her. Childishly Kathryn wanted to stick out her tongue at the broad back and hurl the nearest ornament to hand at the dark head set so assuredly on the strong tanned neck, but he had already pointed out that her behaviour had been childish and she resisted the temptation.

'You bastard!' she spat at him instead, breathing heavily and glaring with loathing at his back.

'I like to think so,' he said casually, turning to face her. 'I certainly can be one when necessary. Now, why don't you pull yourself together, Miss Mallory, and admit defeat. Make up your mind to accept the fact that I'm your new agent and that there's nothing you can do about it. Then we can get on with the job. What do you say?'

'I'll see my solicitor in the morning,' she said, her voice tight with emotion. 'He'll be able to advise me as to what to do. There must be plenty of other pebbles on the beach.'

'Oh, dear, you're very stubborn, Miss Mallory,' he sighed. 'I grant you there may very well be other pebbles on the beach, but I happen to have been chosen for the job by your grandmother. Doesn't that count for anything with you?'

'Kindly leave my grandmother out of it!'

He saw that he had caught her on the raw. 'Impossible, I'm afraid. Surely she's the crux of the whole matter.' Abruptly his tone changed and she knew at once that his words were sincere. 'I regret very much that I never actually met her—by all accounts she was a remarkable old lady. But I did speak to her on the telephone on two occasions and several letters passed between us, and I know that without a doubt it would have been a pleasure and an honour to work for her.'

'But not for me.' The words were out before she had given them any thought.

'That remains to be seen, doesn't it?' They looked at one another wordlessly for what seemed like a considerable time. 'I agree,' Zac Wilding added at length, still holding her eyes with his, 'that, on your showing so far, it would not appear to be a particularly pleasant prospect. But I'm prepared to give it a try.'

'*You're* prepared to give it a try! You really are the most arrogant . . .'

'Now, now!' Maddeningly, he interrupted her in mid-flow. 'We surely don't have to go through all that again. It's excessively boring, don't you think?' His tone was mild but tinged with impatience. 'Make up your mind to it, once and for all, I'm here to stay—for as long as it suits *me*, not you. Now perhaps you will show me to my quarters. Your grandmother said something about a flat over the old stables.'

Taken aback, Kathryn frowned. 'Did she?' She realised with rapidly mounting discomfort that she was becoming increasingly aware of just how cut and dried the arrangements had been between her grandmother and the new agent. 'But no one's lived there for years!'

'I think you'll find,' he said patiently as if he was talking to a child or a halfwit, 'that your grandmother had it made habitable for me. After all, you seem to know very little of what's going on around here. Shall we go and look? I'd like to get settled in.' He walked over to the door and held it open for her. 'Will you lead the way?'

Somehow, without actually having to admit defeat in so many words and still vowing to herself that she would consult Mr Barnes the solicitor first thing in the morning, Kathryn walked through the door ahead of him, head held high an an effort to retain some vestiges of dignity, and wordlessly led the way out of the house and across to the stables. On the way they were joined by Bess, who trotted along beside Zac Wilding, nuzzling his hand every now and then and generally extending a welcome to him, as she did to all and sundry. Really, Kathryn thought crossly, the dog was far too friendly and quite useless as a housedog. She snapped at her to come to heel, but this time, with a swift reproachful glance at her mistress, the dog chose to disobey.

As they approached the stables, Kathryn was almost immediately made aware of the fact that she was about to be made to look a fool yet again. Brightly coloured curtains framed the windows, one of which was slightly ajar, and she even caught sight of a vase of spring flowers on the windowsill, and resignedly she climbed the short flight of bare wooden stairs, certain now that they were about to discover a nicely furnished and well-equipped flat, knowing that Gran would have provided her new agent with good living accommodation if that had been part of the contract between them.

'This is excellent,' he said from behind her and, with renewed irritation, she saw that he was fondling Bess's ears in the way she loved and that the wretched animal was gazing up at him adoringly. 'Most attractive, wouldn't you say?'

She didn't answer, turning away from him to look round the flat. The white-painted door at the top of the stairs opened directly into the good-sized sitting-room and there was also a bedroom,

kitchen and bathroom, all tastefully furnished.
The sitting-room and bedroom were carpeted in a
good quality hard-wearing haircord and the
kitchen and bathroom floors were covered with
blue and white thermoplastic tiles. There were two
comfortable chintz-coverd armchairs in the sitting-
room as well as a small pine table and two upright
chairs to match. There was even a small white-
painted bookcase to one side of the fireplace,
containing a couple of rows of paperbacks. Gran
appeared to have thought of everything, Kathryn
admitted ruefully, and she herself had known
nothing whatever about it. Suddenly she felt
deeply and bitterly ashamed that she could have
shown so little interest in the past, and she
renewed her private vow to make up for it in the
future.

'I'll leave you to settle in,' she said stiffly,
avoiding his eyes, 'but you must understand that
the arrangement is only temporary.' Then she
looked at her watch. 'I'll have dinner sent over to
you in about an hour.' Then, calling sharply to
Bess and without another word to him, she turned
and went quickly back down the stairs. One thing
at least she was determined on, and that was that
while he was here he would not be taking his meals
with her at the Hall. To her surprise, he followed
her down, and she turned and gave him a quick
glance.

'Got to collect my things from the Red Lion,' he
said by way of explanation. 'You wouldn't care to
drive me over there, would you? I take it you do
drive?'

A small smile lit her face as she regarded him.
'Yes, I do drive,' she answered, enjoying her petty

triumph. 'And no, I would not care to take you to the Red Lion. The walk will do you good.' And she turned on her heel, expecting to catch sounds of anger from behind her, but disappointed when all she heard was the sound of gentle mocking laughter, to be followed by the words which neatly turned the tables on her.

'In that case, I'll take the dog. She'll be company for me.'

The next day Kathryn received a telephone call from Mr Barnes, asking if he might call on her that afternoon in order to acquaint her with the terms of her grandmother's will, and accordingly he arrived promptly at the appointed time and was shown into the library, where Kathryn was waiting for him. She was glad that his timely arrival would also give her the opportunity to consult him as to how she could legally get rid of the new agent, but in the event she was so shattered by what the old man had to tell her that they never got round to discussing Zac at all.

After greeting her and settling himself in a chair facing hers, the old family solicitor cleared his throat and said: 'I think you'd better prepare yourself for something of a shock, Kathryn. The terms of your grandmother's will are, shall we say, a trifle unusual? But believe me, my dear, although I did not wholeheartedly approve of her decision, I can assure you that she had only your best interests at heart. I know I don't need to tell you that you were all your grandmother cared about, you and Woollerson Hall and the estate, that is, and although of course she intended that it should all pass to you, there is one rather curious stipulation in her will.'

'You mean there's some doubt that I'm to have Woollerson?' Kathryn interrupted, aghast at the totally unexpected news that the will contained anything out of the ordinary. 'For goodness' sake read the will, Mr Barnes!' Although she had known and liked the old man all her life, just at that moment she could have shaken him in her impatience for him to get to the point.

He held up his hand. 'If you will allow me, Kathryn,' he said a little reproachfully, 'that is exactly what I'm about to do. I was simply trying to prepare you a little, that was all.' Looking slightly ruffled, he glanced down at the document in his hand and with difficulty Kathryn remained silent. She almost groaned aloud when he dropped the will on to his lap and took off his glasses, but she gripped her hands together and waited for him to come to the point in his own good time. 'I think perhaps I'll tell you in my own words,' he said at length, 'and then read the will to you. The nub of the matter, my dear Kathryn, is . . .' maddeningly, he paused again, then leant forward, making a pyramid of his old arthritic hands and resting his scraggy old chin on them as he looked sternly at her, 'that you get Woollerson Hall and the whole of the estate, lock, stock and barrel, if . . .' he stopped and she watched as his Adam's apple rose and fell as he swallowed, 'if you marry within one year from the day of your grandmother's death,' he finished with a rush. Then he sat back with evident relief at having got the words out at last, as Kathryn drew in her breath in a horrified gasp and the colour flamed in her face, then drained away, leaving her unnaturally pale.

'She can't have said that!' she said faintly. 'Oh, surely she wouldn't do a thing like that!'

'I'm afraid so, my dear,' the old man said symathetically. 'She wanted to see you settled at Woollerson Hall, happily married . . .'

'But how can I conveniently arrange to be "happily married" within a year!' Kathryn cried bitterly. 'Things just don't happen like that! Oh, how could she!'

'I discussed the matter with your grandmother on several occasions, my dear, but she was adamant. She said that this was just what you needed to make you face up to your responsibilities and settle down. Naturally, she hoped to see you married before she died, in which case the will would have been re-drawn, but in the event of her death before your marriage, this was her decision. She seemed to think that a year was sufficient time . . .'

'But it's ridiculous—and cruel! It isn't nearly long enough! And what will happen if I don't manage to get myself married off within a year? What happens to Woollerson then?' Angry and bitter although she undoubtedly was, she was in no way prepared for the old man's shattering answer.

'Should you not marry within the year,' he said slowly, fixing her with a pair of lugubrious eyes, 'then Woollerson Hall and the whole of the estate will be sold and the proceeds will go to charity.'

CHAPTER TWO

'WOOLLERSON HALL sold!' Suddenly Kathryn slumped down in her chair. 'Oh, my God, I can't let that happen!' She buried her head in her hands. 'Oh, Gran, what are you trying to do to me?' she muttered.

When old Mr Barnes had left, telling her gently that he would see himself out, she remained sitting where she was while she struggled to regain her composure and collect her thoughts into some sort of order. Nothing had prepared her for the shock she had just received and her mind was in turmoil. She must have sat there for nearly an hour, gradually working her way to a solution, discarding this idea, considering that, until eventually she straightened in her chair, her mind made up. 'I'll do it!' she said out loud. 'I'll damn well do it!'

There was a lot of her grandmother in Kathryn, and once her mind was made up she was not the girl to let the grass grow under her feet, and she therefore crossed swiftly to the telephone and rang the riding stables. Brian was out with some pupils, so she booked herself for an hour's hacking in half an hour's time, telling the stable boy that she hoped Mr Brian would be free to accompany her. Then she went upstairs and changed into riding kit and drove to the stables, arriving in time to see Brian ride in with his pupils.

Soon she was mounted on her favourite chestnut

31

mare, with Brian beside her on his bay, and looking up at him she thought how handsome he was with his thick fair hair blown by the wind and his face aglow from his recent ride. It was a beautiful spring day, and in spite of the events of the past week Kathryn's heart lifted as they trotted out of the yard and down the lane. Perhaps everything was going to be all right, she thought, and Woollerson Hall would be safe. After all, she already loved Brian and he'd told her often enough that he loved her too, so why did she have this sinking sensation in the pit of her stomach? She only had to put it to him tactfully and at the right moment and all would be well.

She chose her moment carefully. After an exhilarating gallop across open country they stopped to give the horses a breather. Sitting in the saddle, she looked out across the magnificent view before them, thinking how unbearable it would be if she ever had to leave. She turned to Brian, her face slightly flushed from the gallop. 'Whenever I come here, I think this must be the most beautiful place in the world,' she said. 'Particularly when I'm with you.'

He smiled across at her. 'You certainly look a bit less peaky today,' he observed. 'Feeling better?' His tone was perfectly normal and she relaxed a little.

'Yes, I think so. The shock's beginning to wear off. But, Brian——' she paused, taking the time to choose her words, 'Mr Barnes came to see me this afternoon, and I must say he gave me a bit of a shock.'

'Oh, what sort of a shock?' Was it her imagination and was she being ultra-sensitive, or had his tone of voice altered subtly? She noticed that his brown eyes did not quite meet hers.

'Under the terms of Gran's will,' she went on slowly, keeping her eyes on his face and determinedly ignoring the sinking feeling within her which was escalating by the second, 'I inherit Woollerson . . .'

'I should jolly well hope so!' he interjected with a kind of false heartiness which she didn't fail to notice.

'Yes, but Brian, there's an "if"—a very big "if". I get Woollerson if I marry within a year of Gran's death.' The moment the words were out and hanging explosively in the air between them and she saw the shock in his eyes, she wished with all her heart that she had never uttered them. It was most definitely not the reaction she had been looking for, and she turned abruptly and, digging her heels into the mare's sides, moved off sharply, calling back over her shoulder, 'Ridiculous, isn't it? Quite absurd! I'll find a way round it. I've no intention of getting married for ages yet.' But as she rode she felt the tears begin to sting her eyes and soon her vision was so blurred that she had to trust the mare to find the way without her guidance. 'Oh, God, what am I going to do now!' she thought desperately. She couldn't risk raising her hand to wipe away the tears, because she could hear Brian close behind her and her pride would not let him see how much he had hurt her.

She had regained her composure by the time they arrived back at the stables, and as Brian helped her to dismount she was able to take his proffered hand without flinching. She even managed to smile up at him as she handed him the

mare's reins. 'Thanks for the ride, Brian. It did me
the world of good. I must come down again later
in the week.' She was, however, merely making
conversation to get her over an awkward moment
and was convinced that nothing on earth would
ever persuade her to set foot in the place again.

She saw the colour suddenly heighten in Brian's
face as he turned and pretended to adjust the girth
on the bay. 'I'm booked up completely for the rest
of the week with beginners, Kathryn,' he said.
'Perhaps . . .'

'Oh, I wouldn't expect you to come with me!'
she said quickly, only just managing to keep a note
of scorn out of her voice. 'I'm perfectly all right on
my own.' And she walked briskly over to where
her car was parked and soon she was speeding
away down the lane with a cheery wave for Brian,
but it cost her every ounce of self-control and as
soon as she was out of sight she pulled in to the
side, because she found that she was shaking and
she didn't want to risk an accident. What had
happened to Brian? she asked herself as she
struggled to pull herself together. Why hadn't he
immediately asked her to marry him? Everything
would have been all right if he had and her worries
would have been over. It didn't take her long to
come to the humiliating conclusion that probably
he'd never been in love with her at all and that it
had all been on her side.

When she had recovered, she drove slowly back
to the Hall, her last words to Brian echoing
hollowly in her mind. 'I'm perfectly all right on my
own,' she had said, but just at that moment she
felt that her brave statement couldn't have been
much farther removed from the truth. Now that

Brian had turned out to be a broken reed, she felt more alone than ever, and it was with a heavy heart that she went indoors and threw herself into an armchair in the drawing-room, her face flaming with embarrassment when she thought of the way she had offered herself to Brian and been rejected. She buried her face in her hands and groaned aloud. Had Gran guessed all along that he wouldn't come up to scratch? she wondered. Oh, wise old Gran! But what was she to do now? Brian had been her only hope. Why had he told her he loved her so often in the past? Hadn't he expected her to take him seriously? Now she felt she almost hated him. Everything was spoiled. Her first and only romance was over. 'Oh, Gran,' she whispered, 'are you sure you knew what you were doing? Did you really want things to turn out like this?'

As she sat on in the drawing-room, her mind racing up one blind alley after another, her mood gradually began to change. The state of shock brought about by Mr Barnes' pronouncements had worn off, and as for the humiliating blow dealt her by Brian, she knew that this was something she would have to live with until time eventually eroded the hurt and it became nothing more than an unpleasant memory and something which could be dismissed as an unfortunate experience brought about mainly by a lack of experience in the ways of the world and of men in particular. The fighting spirit of the Mallorys was beginning to reassert itself, and she jumped to her feet and strode over to the door. She saw from her watch that there was an hour before dinner and, going out into the hall and taking a jacket from the row of heavy old brass hooks by the door, she went out into the cool evening air, the old dog lumbering faithfully after her. A walk would do her good and help clear her head; it always did, and there was no reason why today should be any exception. She knew that for the time being she would have to blot Brian out of her mind; the hurt was too new and her feelings too raw. She forgave herself her earlier tears but resolved that there should be no more. Love and all its attendant hang-ups could take a running jump, she decided. It was altogether too risky a business, and she vowed that it would be a very long time before she allowed her heart to stray again from her own safe keeping.

She walked a short distance down the drive, then cut off to the right until she came out on to the sweeping expanse of lawn in front of the house, then continued over the grass towards the kissing gate which gave access from the immediate grounds to the open parkland beyond. The grass was wet and had recently received its first cutting of the season and her shoes were soon soaked and smothered in grass cuttings. Bess happily padded along beside her and, as soon as they were through the kissing gate, set off in pursuit of a rabbit, whose white scut was just disappearing into the undergrowth. Kathryn smiled as the old dog came panting back to her, grinning all over her face, her tail waving in appreciation of the outing, then she bent and stroked the warm silky head. 'You're getting slow, old girl,' she said. 'You'll never catch one at that rate. Look, over there!'

Bess turned and lumbered off in the general direction indicated by Kathryn's pointing finger to where several more rabbits were hopping about unconcernedly in the last of the sunshine. Even when they became aware of the dog bearing down upon them they seemed to take their time before eventually scuttling off, as if they knew that she was getting past it and no longer posed any real threat to their safety. Kathryn leant against the old iron fencing, idly watching Bess's antics, but her mind was far away and she jumped like a startled fawn at the sudden and unwelcome sound of a man's voice behind her.

'I wouldn't encourage her if I were you. She could drop dead. She's grossly overweight.'

Her mouth tightened in irritation as she turned and regarded the tall figure standing a few feet from her, hands thrust deep into the pockets of a pair of old faded cords, dark hair only slightly ruffled by the breeze, blue eyes boring into her as penetratingly as ever. Altogether he looked thoroughly at home, she noted sourly, very much as if he belonged and had been part of the scenery for a long time, instead of a bare twenty-four hours.

'Why don't you mind your own business?' she said rudely. 'Bess is none of your concern.'

'I don't like to see a dog that's too fat,' Zac Wilding returned imperturbably, then he bent to stroke the old dog who had spied him and come floundering through the long grass to extend her usual exuberant greeting. 'Good girl,' he said. 'Down! That's enough. I said down!' To Kathryn's increased irritation, Bess obeyed him at once, quite naturally, as if he had as much right as she to issue orders, and lay panting at his feet, gazing adoringly up at him for all the world as if he were her lord and master. 'You see,' he said, nudging

Bess with the toe of his heavy rubber boot. 'Look at her! All that extra weight can't be good for her. It puts too great a strain on the heart. You must be overfeeding her or she's not getting enough exercise.'

'She certainly gets enough exercise,' Kathryn retorted, stung by his criticism. 'But I really don't know about her food. Cook feeds her, and I daresay she gets the odd titbit in the kitchen.'

'Do you mean to say,' he said, turning and giving her a look compounded of disgust and disbelief, 'that you don't see to her food yourself? Just what *do* you do around here? Precious little, so far as I can see.'

'How dare you!' Kathryn was so angry she could have hit him. 'It's absolutely none of your business what I do or don't do. And as for Bess, the servants adore her and look after her perfectly adequately.'

'In my experience servants always spoil dogs and should be allowed to have as little to do with them as possible,' he returned smoothly. 'But of course, as you so rightly point out, that really is none of my business.' He straightened, taking his hands out of his pockets. 'I'll be on my way. Good evening, Miss Mallory.' Then he paused and looked back at her. 'Unless you'd like me to take the dog back to the house for you. I've got the Land Rover in the lane.' As soon as he had made a move, the old dog had got stiffly to her feet, evidently intent on following him.

'My goodness, you really have settled in, haven't you.' Kathryn's voice was heavy with sarcasm. 'And what about poor Mr Eliot? What's he supposed to do now that you've commandeered his transport?'

'I dropped him off on my way back, of course. Did you really think I'd leave the old boy stranded?' It was evident that he did not intend that her words should disturb his equilibrium one jot. 'Come on, old girl,' he added, bending down and giving Bess a friendly slap, 'it's time someone took you in hand before it's too late.'

'Just a minute!' Kathryn's voice rang out in the evening stillness. 'I never accepted your offer of a lift for Bess. Kindly remember that she's *my* dog. I won't have you taking her over like this!' She felt herself becoming hot with temper as she glared at him.

With an impatient shrug of his shoulders he started to walk away. 'Very well, Miss Mallory, if you're really so sure you know what you're doing. But don't come running to me when the poor dog drops dead.'

'What on earth makes you think I would come running to you? I can assure you, you would be the very last person I would turn to—under any circumstances. Bess—come here!' Her last words were issued on an almost hysterical yell as, furiously, she watched the poor animal trotting away from her with her new-found friend.

Dog and man turned to face her together, and at the look in Bess's eyes she wanted to run to her and reassure the bewildered animal that her anger was not directed at her, but she stood her ground, defiantly outstaring the domineering male facing her.

'Of course Bess must do as you say, Miss Mallory,' he said evenly, 'but I'm truly amazed that you should put your pride before the wellbeing of an animal for whom you evidently feel very little responsibility. I will leave her to your tender loving care.' He turned and when Bess made a further move to follow him, said quietly: 'Stay, girl. Now go to your mistress.' And as the dog slowly obeyed, he watched her waddling over the grass towards Kathryn and added: 'But I do suggest that you take a good look at her and put her on a strict diet at once—or should I say give instructions to Cook to put her on a diet, since it's apparently beneath you actually to see to the matter yourself? It's exactly the same as for a human, you know. It's dangerous for anyone to be grossly overweight—it puts a strain on one's whole system. Not, I grant you,' he added suddenly, pausing and looking her slowly up and down, 'that you can ever have had that problem.'

Almost choking with rage at his insolence, Kathryn turned her back on him and, summoning up every ounce of self-control that she possessed, managed to walk casually away from him, at the same time noting with enormous relief that Bess was following her and was not about to make a fool of her again. Only when she heard the sound of the Land Rover's engine fading into the distance did she allow herself to relax. Then she climbed up on to the old iron fence which ran either side of the kissing gate and sat there for a good ten minutes in order to give Bess time to rest. Although she would have died rather than admit it, Zac Wilding had succeeded in worrying her about the old dog and she knew that, however much she disliked the idea of following his advice, she was going to have to do something about it. The thought of losing Bess was appalling and she cursed herself aloud for her thoughtlessness. She also took pleasure in roundly cursing Zac as well for being the one to point it out to her.

During the next few days Kathryn made sure that she did not bump into Zac again. She also took Bess to the vet in the nearby market town of Haversham, returning laden with vitamin pills, a diet sheet and a great deal of advice on how to bring Bess back to peak condition and thereby ensure that she be allowed to live out her allotted span. The vet had treated her in very much the same way as Zac—like a thoughtless child, she fumed silently. But she had the grace to admit, albeit privately, that both men had been right. To her immense relief, Bess appeared to be basically in good health and the vet assured her that if his instructions were rigidly adhered to, she should live for a few more years at least.

'I'm glad you had the good sense to come and see me when you did, Miss Mallory,' he said as he showed her out, 'before your servants had ruined her health completely.' Kathryn had the grace to blush at his words, having shamelessly put the greater part of the blame for Bess's condition on to Cook's spoiling. 'I think you'll find it better to take charge of her feeding yourself. Perhaps you could arrange to feed her away from the kitchen— and of course you must give strict instructions that she's not to be given any scraps or titbits whatever.' She was aware of the reproof in his voice, although he was too polite to make it too obvious. 'We'll soon have her fit again if you do as I say. Bring her back in about a month and we'll see how much she's improved.'

Kathryn slowly walked back to the car with

Bess waddling along beside her. With a new clarity, she looked down at her and realised that 'waddling' was the appropriate word, and she vowed silently that, although it was going to be hard and particularly so because of course the dog would not understand why all her little extras had suddenly been withdrawn, she was going to follow the vet's advice to the letter.

When she reached the car she unlocked the tailgate and tossed the packets of pills the vet had given her over on to the front seat, then, with a hefty shove, helped Bess up into the back. Then, briskly turning the key in the lock once more, she took a deep breath and set off for her next appointment. There was a grim little smile hovering round her lips as she walked swiftly through the small town until she came to the rather austere-looking building which housed the offices of most of the professional firms in the area, including those of Barnes, Barnes & Wainwright, Solicitors.

'I want to know if I can get rid of Mr Wilding,' she said, coming straight to the point as soon as she was seated in old Mr Barnes' office. 'I'm afraid he's really quite unsuitable and will have to be replaced. I've come to you, rather than dismissing him out of hand, because I wondered what my legal position would be, should he be unwilling to leave. Having been actually taken on by my grandmother, have I the right to fire him? I'm sure I must be able to, but I wanted to make quite sure.'

'My dear Kathryn,' Mr Barnes frowned and there was a distinctly puzzled expression in his faded blue eyes, 'you do surprise me. Mr Eliot speaks of Mr Wilding in the most glowing of terms.'

'Oh, really?' She was taken aback but determined not to show it. 'But how can Mr Eliot possibly tell in such a short time?' Too late she saw the trap into which she had fallen.

'Precisely, my dear.' Mr Barnes smiled kindly at her, but she suddenly realised that he probably was not the doddering old fool she had always affectionately thought him. 'He's evidently got off to a bad start with you, if not with Mr Eliot, but why don't you give him a little longer? He can only be feeling his way for the moment. Give him time to find his feet. Don't you think that would be fair?'

Temporarily at a loss, Kathryn sat and stared back at him, thinking bitterly that there seemed to be a conspiracy against her of late, but knowing in her heart that her reasons for wanting to get rid of her new agent were purely personal and had nothing whatever to do with his competence, or lack of it, in the job to which her grandmother had appointed him.

'There's another point which I think you would do well to consider,' Mr Barnes added. 'If you were to dismiss him after so short a time, I fear it might destroy or at least damage local confidence in you. As I'm sure you're aware, in a small community such as ours, word travels quickly, and I fear you might find it difficult to find a replacement. In any case, it would take time, and you really can't afford to be without an agent, can you? No, my dear.' He stood up, making it plain that the interview was at an end. 'Take my advice and give him a little longer. I'm sure you'll change your mind about him in a few months.'

A few months! Kathryn repeated the words furiously to herself as she stalked back to where she had parked the car. The thought of a few months with that arrogant, overbearing, presumptuous man about the place made her blood boil. She would change her solicitor! Find someone who would do what she asked for a change, someone who wouldn't bring an interview to an end until she was good and ready. She knew that old Mr Barnes would never have treated her grandmother in such a manner.

Angrily jingling the car keys in her hand, head bent as she made her way through the town, her thoughts were venomous as she searched grimly for a way to get rid of Zac without losing face and making life more difficult for herself in the process. Then she whirled round, startled and annoyed, as her arm was suddenly seized from behind and an all too familiar voice assailed her ears.

'Miss Mallory! Didn't you hear me? I've been calling your name for some time. What a bit of luck running into you!'

With resignation and disdain, she turned and looked stonily up at the one man in all the world she could have hoped not to bump into at that moment. 'Mr Wilding,' she said, standing still and regarding him with intense dislike. 'What do you want now?'

He looked back at her for a second, then suddenly burst into a shout of laughter. 'From your expression and with my amazing intelligence I could hazard a guess that you were thinking about me. I'm sure no one else has quite that effect on you. Am I right?'

'Right!' she snapped. She realised that people were staring at them and started to walk on. 'What did you want? I'm in a hurry.' She quickened her pace and he moved round behind her until he was walking on the outside and then took her arm once more.

'Allow me to escort you to wherever you're going,' he said, tightening his grip as she tried to shake him off.

'I'm going back to the car,' she said from between clenched teeth. 'And please leave go of my arm.'

'I'm only exercising my impeccable manners. I was very well brought up, you know. Also, I hoped you were going to your car—that was why I was so glad to see you. I'm sure you didn't imagine I was pleased to see you for yourself. I had to bring the Land Rover into the garage. It conked out on me this morning and I had the devil's own job getting it going again. I'm afraid it's pretty well clapped out. You'll have to think about getting a new one.'

They had reached her car now and she stopped and looked up at him. 'Will you stop giving me orders, Mr Wilding,' she said with what she considered quite admirable calm. 'I shall decide if and when we need a new Land Rover—as I shall decide anything and everything else of any importance. Kindly remember that I'm the boss.'

For a split second she saw a glint of steel in his eyes as the mask of flippancy slipped. 'Very well, Miss Mallory,' he said tightly, 'if that's the way you want it.'

'Oh, it is,' she said. 'It most certainly is. Now, if you don't mind, I have to get back.'

'Of course,' he said, relaxing, 'but I need a lift. Didn't you realise that was why I ran after you back there? Or were you so engrossed in your thoughts that you didn't take in what I said about the Land Rover? I'm afraid it's going to be out of action for a few days. Of course if you really find my company so offensive, I could hire a car and charge it up to you. But it would involve rather a lot of unnecessary expense.'

Kathryn closed her eyes for a moment while she struggled to maintain her outward calm, then walked round and unlocked the driver's door. 'Get in!' she muttered from between clenched teeth, realising that she really had no alternative to driving him back to Woollerson. Then she saw the pills the vet had given her for Bess lying on the passenger seat where she had thrown them, and she picked them up and hastily crammed them into her bag, before getting in and leaning across and unlocking the passenger door. The sudden grin on Zac's face told her that she had not been quick enough, but he made no comment, merely contenting himself with greeting the dog, who was making welcoming noises and trying to get at him from her place at the back of the car.

Apparently perfectly at ease, Zac lounged in the seat beside her as she started the car and pulled somewhat jerkily away from the kerb. 'Been driving long?' he asked casually, but she sensed the criticism and did not reply. Instead she increased her speed to a level bordering on the dangerous as they sped through the narrow streets and out into the open country beyond the town 'What's the hurry?' he asked mildly, as she kept her foot hard down on the accelerator. Then he laughed. 'I'll bet you're just itching to get back home so that you can stick another pin into the little image you've made of me!' He slumped even further down into his seat, as she took a corner much too fast and he was in danger of being thrown against her. 'Good job I don't get carsick. Let me know when we're there, will you?' And he closed his eyes and leant his head against the back of the seat.

Once his eyes were closed and she felt that his attention was no longer focused on her Kathryn did slow down a little, knowing that she was being foolish in allowing her intense irritation and urgent wish to be rid of him as quickly as possible to affect her driving. An accident now would solve nothing. She shot him a brief glance, then looked away again quickly for fear he would suddenly open those disturbing blue eyes of his and find her looking at him. Whether in repose as he was now, or when he was in the midst of one of his scathingly critical attacks on herself, the chief impression she got of the large, intensely masculine individual currently lounging beside her was one of immense strength, physical and mental, and of an iron will which she knew would be a constant challenge, an ever-present goad, which would bedevil her whole future if she were not to get rid of him quickly. Somehow, she told herself grimly, no matter what underhand means she might be forced to employ in order to achieve her objective, somehow and some time soon she would send him packing!

When she turned the car into the drive and it crunched its way over the gravel as it sped towards the house, Zac sat up and opened his eyes. 'You're a good driver when you're not in a temper,' he said pleasantly, stretching his arms out in front of him. 'Thanks for the lift—boss.' Then, almost before she had stopped the car, he had got out and come round to hold her door open for her. He acknowledged her terse thanks with a brief smile, before taking the keys from her and letting the dog out of the back, and he watched without comment as Bess scrambled in an ungainly stumbling jump down on to the gravel. 'By the way,' he said as he strolled back to where she was still standing beside the car, 'I'll need your car for a few days, if it's all right with you. Until the Land Rover is ready.' He still held the keys in his hand and he tossed them up into the air and caught them again several times while she watched, understanding him perfectly, determined that on this occasion she would not rise to his bait.

'Certainly you may borrow my car, Mr Wilding,' Kathryn replied evenly, 'when I don't need it myself. I'll let you know when it's available.' She was damned if she was going to give him the satisfaction of making her ask for the keys. There was a spare set in the house and she would use them when the necessity arose.

Zac smiled and she thought she detected in his glance an acknowledgment of the fact that she had for once managed to keep her temper under his provocation. 'Why don't you keep horses any more? The stables are still in very good condition. Then I could have ridden round the estate.'

'When my grandmother became too old to ride any more, she decided that the expense wasn't justified,' she replied grudgingly. 'I wasn't one of those horse-mad girls, and in any case I was away at boarding school, and when I wanted to ride in the holidays I could always go to the riding school the other side of the village. I still ride occasionally,' she added bleakly.

He seemed about to say something more, but she had a feeling that he had picked up the sudden sadness in her voice and decided to keep whatever it was to himself. 'Perhaps we could ride together some time,' he said unexpectedly and surprisingly gently. 'When I can take some time off.'

'Perhaps,' she was startled into replying, all at once feeling very vulnerable and miserable. For a moment she felt disarmed, but it did not last and she reminded herself how much she disliked the man as she quickly went into the house, leaving him still standing beside the car. Once inside she leant for a moment against the closed front door, puzzled to find that for some unknown reason she felt strangely disturbed and that her heartbeat was a little faster than normal. Could it be simply because he had spoken to her kindly? she wondered, frowning. But how absurd! The wretched man meant less than nothing to her, in fact was an obvious and definite thorn in her side and if she was to allow herself to be affected by a few kind words from a man like him, then things had indeed come to a pretty pass and the sooner she pulled herself together the better!

With a sigh, she moved away from the door and made for the library. She had received literally dozens of letters of condolence on Gran's death and had so far made very little headway in dealing with them, but she was determined to answer each one personally and she spent the rest of the day on them, emerging bleary-eyed and exhausted at around five o'clock, with the satisfaction of a large pile of neatly addressed envelopes to show for her labours, symmetrically stacked on the large old desk. She found that she hadn't enough stamps for all of them and silently chided herself for having omitted to buy some when she was in Haversham.

Deciding to go down to the post office in the village, she gathered up the pile of envelopes in her arms and took them out to the car, which was still parked outside. She put them on the passenger seat, then went back to get some money for the stamps, returning in what could only have been a few minutes to see the car disappearing down the drive, with the hated and quite unmistakable figure of Zac at the wheel. Furiously she dashed out on to the drive, shouting impotently after the retreating car, railing at him at the top of her voice, almost beside herself with anger. Then to her amazement she saw the rear lights come on, glowing red as Zac applied the brakes, and in a moment she saw that he was backing the car rapidly up the drive until it was right beside where she was standing, whereupon Zac leapt out and strode round to her.

'I do apologise,' he said, to her astonishment. 'I thought you wouldn't be needing the car again today. I was just nipping down to the village and had then intended to put it away for you. Don't look so disbelieving—I assure you I wasn't trying to be clever.'

'But you could see all those letters on the seat,' she said accusingly. 'Why on earth did you think I'd put them there? Surely even you could work it out that I was taking them down to the village post office.'

'I saw them, of course,' he said with an

impatient sigh. 'I'm sorry, I just didn't think. Would you like me to post them for you?'

'No, thank you, I think I can just about manage it on my own. Anyway, I need some more stamps. Excuse me.' She tried to slip past him and into the driver's seat, but he was too quick for her.

'I could get the stamps for you,' he said, getting into the driver's seat himself, 'but if you insist on doing it yourself, get in. I'll drive you down.'

For an instant Kathryn struggled to bite back an angry retort then, having succeeded in achieving a fragile control of her anger, made her way round to the passenger seat and began gathering up the letters before getting in beside him in as dignified a manner as possible. 'How very kind of you,' she said, her voice positively oozing with odium. 'Are you sure it isn't too much trouble?'

Zac looked straight ahead without speaking for a moment and she looked down and saw that his hands were gripping the wheel so hard that the knuckles showed white through the brown skin. Then he turned to look at her and their eyes locked. But when he spoke all he said was: 'Quite sure, Miss Mallory. It's no trouble at all.'

When her business at the post office was completed and she came out into the rather chill evening air once more, she found Zac standing waiting for her, and when he saw her he approached and, putting his hand under her elbow, began to walk her in the direction of the Red Lion. 'Come and have a drink,' he said. 'It's time we got to know one another.'

Immediately she dug in her heels and removed herself from his grasp. 'No, thank you,' she said ungraciously, 'I'd really rather get back.' Then she added maliciously: 'And if you want a drink, then I'm afraid you'll have to walk back, because I intend to take the car. I have to take Bess for her walk.'

As she drove away, leaving him to go into the Red Lion alone, she was uncomfortably aware that her refusal to join him had been unnecessarily churlish, but, having once embarked on her chosen course of antagonism, she found it almost impossible to change her attitude and her refusal had been instinctive.

When she reached the house she whistled up the old dog, and soon the two of them were making their way over the lawns and down towards the kissing gate and she admitted to herself that her reason for taking the same walk as on the previous day was in the knowlege that this was the most direct route to and from the village and that Zac would in all probability come back this way. She resolved that, should he do so, she would make an effort to be a little more pleasant to him, knowing very well that her grandmother would not have approved in the least of her recent rudeness. But fate decreed that she was not to be given this opportunity, and although she lingered on for some time in the meadow beyond the old iron palings, he did not appear, and eventually she and Bess made their way slowly back to the house.

After her solitary dinner, Kathryn wandered into the drawing-room and idly switched on the television. She knew that she was heartily sick of her own company but didn't really know what she could do about it. Now that it was too late, she deeply regretted having more or less dropped most of her friends when she had fallen in love with Brian. Once she had, in her inexperience and almost total ignorance of such matters, decided that she loved him, he had seemed to fill her whole life and she had felt no need of anyone's company but his. Now that her love affair was over there was an enormous void in a life which had always had rather narrow margins but which had seemed full and satisfying to her, and she wondered, desperately and hopelessly, where on earth she was going to find herself a husband.

She spent a thoroughly boring evening, ostensibly watching television but taking in very little, her thoughts always returning to her great problem, the enormity of which seemed to be increasing as the days sped past. She had never been particularly aware before that time was passing either exceptionally quickly or exceptionally slowly, but now all that was changed and already her one precious year appeared to be running out as quickly and inexorably as the grains of sand in an hourglass.

After she had watched the news she decided that, although it was a little earlier than usual, she would put Bess out for her last night amble round the grounds and then go to bed and read. The mere fact of having made a concrete plan cheered her up, and she went out into the hall and whistled. The dog normally appeared almost at once, but this evening was an exception, and Kathryn hunted high and low for her, calling and whistling and eventually opening the front door and going out into the pitch darkness, calling as she went.

There was no moon, only a million stars in the

black sky above her head, and she walked slowly away from the house until her eyes began to adjust to the almost total lack of light. She walked a little way round towards the back of the house where a sudden brilliant shaft of light pierced the gloom, and she stopped with an exclamation. The light was coming from the flat above the old stables and her instincts told her that without very much doubt Bess was with Zac.

'Damn his cheek!' she said out loud, and she stalked angrily over the gravel, then up the bare wooden stairs and rapped sharply on the white-painted door at the top. One short bark from inside confirmed her suspicion and her lips tightened as Zac opened the door. 'I've come for Bess,' she said curtly before he could say anything. She looked past him at the dog who hadn't even bothered to get up at the sound of her mistress's voice, but who contented herself with lying in a large golden heap up against the chair which had just been vacated by Zac, her tail thumping rhythmically on the carpet in welcome. 'Come on, girl, time to go.'

Kathryn turned preparatory to descending the stairs once more, hoping grimly that Bess would follow, and was completely taken by surprise when she felt her arm seized in a hard grip as Zac pulled her roughly into the room. 'Come in and have a nightcap,' he said, retaining his grasp on her arm as he felt her instinctively trying to free herself.

'No, thanks,' she said stiffly. 'I'll just take Bess and go.'

'It wasn't an invitation,' he said easily, pulling her abruptly farther into the room and shutting the door firmly behind her. 'It was an order.' He laughed as she opened her mouth to reply. 'Save your breath, my dear girl,' he added. 'I already know you well enough to appreciate that a request gets an automatic "no" from you. An order seems to be the only alternative. I suppose you're one of those women who secretly like to be dominated by a man.'

'Don't be ridiculous!'

'It doesn't bother me in the least, one way or the other,' he went on, ignoring her words. 'So long as we both know where we stand. Now, what about that drink? What would you like?'

Although his superior attitude maddened her and every instinct told her to make for the door, she was under no illusion as to her ability to get there before him, since he appeared to be watching her with peculiar concentration from the brilliant blue eyes. She was also remembering her earlier wish to make amends for her rudeness, and she therefore sat down abruptly in the armchair opposite his, feeling suddenly absurdly grateful when Bess got stiffly to her feet and came and collapsed with a sigh of contentment beside her. 'I don't really want a drink, thank you,' she said, looking quickly up at Zac and then away again. 'I don't drink very much, actually.'

'Would you prefer coffee? It won't take a minute.'

She could feel his eyes still on her as she nodded without looking up this time. 'Yes, please, that would be nice.'

He disappeared, returning in a few minutes with two cups. 'Thought I'd join you,' he said, handing hers to her. 'Sugar?' They sipped their coffee in silence for a few minutes, then, very deliberately,

Zac put down his cup and leant forward. 'Don't you think it's time we buried the hatchet?' he asked quietly. 'I'm sure you'll agree it's ridiculous to go on like this.' He looked at her expectantly, but when she didn't answer he sighed and tapped his foot impatiently. 'Look,' his tone was suddenly hard and uncompromising, 'I know you're still trying to get rid of me, so you needn't bother to deny it.'

'I wasn't going to,' Kathryn said flatly, and saw the rueful downturning of the corners of his mouth.

'No, of course not. Believe me, I don't underestimate you for one minute, but is all this antagonism really necessary? Aren't you being a bit paranoid about me? Just what is it you have against me?'

Once again she didn't answer. Cornered and completely at a loss for words, she looked back into his hard blue eyes and was the first to look away.

Suddenly he laughed. 'You see?' he said with mild triumph. 'You can't really answer, can you? You don't have to like me, you know. It's beside the point. I can still do a good job for you here, even if you hate the sight of me. It really doesn't matter to me one way or the other. But I don't mind admitting that I've fallen in love with this place and I want to stay. All I'm asking is that you give me a fair trial. I have great plans for the estate which I want to discuss with you, but it's pointless if you won't even listen. What I'm asking is that we leave personalities out of it and get on with the job together. We could do great things here together. What do you say?'

Kathryn looked steadily back at him, knowing that this time she would have to give him an answer, and all at once, for some unknown reason, she was able to see the situation between them through his eyes and realised all too clearly how stupid and prejudiced her attitude was. She cleared her throat and with a supreme effort managed a small and rather forced smile. 'Yes, all right,' she said quietly. 'We'll give it a try.'

She was immediately rewarded with a genuine and very broad grin on the handsome face of the dynamic man sitting opposite her, and when he leant forward and gripped her hand in a strong firm handshake, for once she didn't try to pull away. 'Good girl!' he said, the smile reaching his eyes. 'I knew you'd see it my way in the end.'

'Don't spoil things by getting too pleased with yourself,' she said, laughing a little shakily as she got up to go. 'We'll still have to see how it works out.'

'Being a woman, of course you had to have the last word,' he said on a mock sigh as he too stood up and went to open the door for her. 'Goodnight, Kathryn. I'll see you in the morning.' Then he called to the dog, who was still lying blissfully asleep by the chair Kathryn had just vacated. 'Come on, old girl, go with your mistress.'

Kathryn went down the stairs and called 'Goodnight' without looking back at Zac and, with Bess padding along behind her, walked back to the house in the darkness, aware of an odd little spark of pleasure which she had unexpectedly experienced when Zac had called her by her Christian name for the first time. Perhaps things were going to work out with the new agent after all, she thought as she opened the front door and waited for Bess to lumber inside. At any rate, she was now prepared to give it a try.

CHAPTER THREE

ALTHOUGH at first she did not know why, when she awoke next morning Kathryn knew at once that the dead weight which had seemed to be weighing her down since her grandmother's sudden death had considerably lightened. Then she remembered the conversation with Zac the previous evening and suddenly she was fully awake and, throwing back the bedclothes, she jumped out of bed and pulled back the curtains. A gentle rain was falling, but already there was more than a hint of sun in the brightening sky and she smiled as she went through to the bathroom and ran her bath. All at once life held some purpose and she was frankly looking forward to having something to do. She wondered when Zac intended that they should have their talk, and when she went downstairs half an hour later she put her head round the door of what had originally been the morning room but which had for many years been used as the estate office. To her surprise Zac was already there, and when he saw her he stood up with a smile.

'Good morning. Ready? Shall we get down to it right away?'

'It's a bit early, isn't it?' she frowned. 'I didn't

really expect to find you here yet. I haven't had breakfast.'

Now it was his turn to frown as he looked pointedly at his watch. 'I don't call after nine o'clock early, Miss Mallory.' Kathryn was aware of a ridiculous stab of disappointment at his return to formality when addressing her, although at the same time she admitted to herself that she would probably have considered it presumptuous had he called her by her first name. She shook her head, more in irritation with herself than with him and also because she felt that, gainsaying her earlier mood of optimism, the atmosphere between them had not really improved at all.

'I consider nine o'clock to be the civilised hour for people to have breakfast,' she said icily. 'I'll see you later.' She turned to leave, but paused at his next remark.

'Off you go, then,' he said curtly, 'but don't expect to find me here just when it suits you. I've got work to do. When I've gone through the post, I'm off to see old Mr Roberts at the Home Farm, and I shall need your car.'

She turned and faced him, gripping the door handle as if she wanted to crush it in her hand. 'For God's sake, Mr Wilding!' she spat at him, her voice raised until she was almost shouting. 'Why do you always have to be so objectionable!' Then she spun round on her heel and walked out of the room, quite unable to resist slamming the door behind her.

But before she had taken two steps across the hall, the door was yanked open again and Zac strode out into the hall until he was standing in front of her, eyes blazing. Then he seized both her hands in his and shook her. 'What on earth is the matter with you, you stupid girl!' His voice was icy cold and very quiet, which had far more effect than her shouting. 'Have you forgotten our talk of last night? I thought we'd agreed to call a truce.'

A door opened on the far side of the hall and they both turned to see one of the maids staring at them in amazement. Zac released her hands abruptly, but instead of allowing Kathryn to escape, he pushed her none too gently back towards the office. 'In there,' he said with barely controlled anger. 'We'll have this out once and for all!'

Being unwilling to make a scene in front of the maid and after only a moment's hesitation, Kathryn walked defiantly back into the office and marched over to the window, standing with her back to him until she heard him close the door behind him. Then she turned and faced him as he walked purposefully across the room and stood immediately in front of her. 'Now, let's have it,' he said, his tone a mixture of anger and exasperation. 'What's happened since last night to make you go back on your word? I thought we'd come to some sort of understanding, but apparently I was wrong. Go on, tell me!' His eyes were like granite, hard and cold and full of scorn, and it took all Kathryn's resolution not to look away.

'Nothing's happened,' she said belligerently. 'There's nothing new. It's just your whole attitude, your colossal cheek in presuming to order me about. I just won't have it! I can't. . . .' Her voice trailed off as she watched him visibly relax and then, unbelievably, begin to smile. She looked away and then, strangely, felt all her resolve begin to crumble as she suddenly saw herself through his eyes. Her smallness of mind, her petty resentments, her pique whenever he appeared to be taking charge and overstepping his authority – all seemed suddenly incredibly silly and shallow, and she was completely at a loss for words. Then to her utter amazement, she felt rather than saw a pair of strong arms reach out for her and pull her to him as he held her slim figure against his tall hard body.

'You poor kid,' he said, and his voice was more gentle than she would have believed possible. 'Your whole life's been turned upside down and you haven't really got your bearings yet, have you? So you go floundering around trying to assert an authority you haven't really got, taking offence at the slightest thing which could remotely be construed as an insult or a threat to your position – until you're flying at my throat every time I open my mouth. I understand now, so I'll go easy on you. All right, all right, don't start again,' he added as he felt her stir against him. 'That wasn't meant to be patronising. I'm just trying to tell you that I for one am prepared to make allowances.'

'How very kind of you,' she said, recovering somewhat and removing herself from the embrace in which she had so surprisingly found herself. But the words lacked their usual sting and her mind was only half concentrating on what she was saying. She was struggling inwardly to avoid admitting to herself that the feel of his arms clamped firmly round her had been anything but unpleasant. 'You're so understanding.' Try as she would, the sarcasm refused to make itself felt and she even felt the beginnings of a smile hovering not too far away.

'Mind you,' he said softly, 'it's not going to be easy, is it?'

'No,' she agreed as she stared back at him. And then she really did manage a smile, even though it was a trifle rueful. 'It isn't.'

Then Zac held out his right hand to her, as he had the night before and they shook. 'Mean it this time, Kathryn,' he said, briefly joining his other hand so that hers was held in both of his. 'We'll never get anything done if we're pulling in opposite directions.' Then he released her. 'Now go and have your breakfast. I'll wait if you're not too long. Perhaps you'll come with me to the Home Farm?'

Half an hour later she was seated beside him in her car on their way to see Mr Roberts, tenant for as long as she could remember of the Home Farm. Zac had made it perfectly plain that he intended to drive and Kathryn had managed to refrain from protest and had got in beside him with a good grace. Now that she thought about it, she really didn't mind in the least who drove and soon they were deep in conversation about the coming interview with the old farmer.

'Eliot tells me that old Mr Roberts wants to retire but is afraid that if he does he and his wife will have nowhere to live. Apparently there's an empty cottage that they could have, but it isn't in very good shape, so you'll have to agree to spend some money on it before they can move in.'

'Shouldn't we go and have a look at the cottage first, then? It would seem logical.'

'Yes, I agree. But I thought we'd better make sure first that old Roberts really does want to go.'

'But didn't you say Mr Eliot told you he did?'

'I always prefer to find out for myself.'

'Don't you trust anyone?' she asked.

He gave her a brief sidelong glance at her question. 'No. That's one cardinal rule I've learnt. Never trust anyone—especially a woman.'

Kathryn looked at him sharply, noting his suddenly bleak expression. 'Was that directed at me?'

He blinked and she knew that his thoughts had been far away. 'Of course not,' he grunted. 'You haven't given me any reason to mistrust you—yet.'

Wisely deciding not to pursue the matter and sensing his sudden unexplained change of mood, Kathryn subsided into silence and was relieved when they soon drove into the cobbled yard of the Home Farm. Mrs Roberts was her usual rosy welcoming self and took them into the snug and homely kitchen, while a lad was sent to fetch her husband. Zac appeared to have regained his equilibrium and soon the four of them were seated in front of the old black-leaded range with steaming mugs of tea in their hands as they discussed the old couple's retirement.

Having established that the Roberts's did indeed wish to retire, when they left, Zac and Kathryn drove straight on to view the empty cottage, which, to Kathryn's unpractised eye appeared to be in very poor shape indeed. But as Zac took her from room to room, pointing out what would need to be done and telling her roughly what it would cost, a new respect for him began to grow in her and an assured confidence in him was born. 'You really know what you're talking about, don't you?' she found herself saying, when they were back in the car once more preparatory to returning to the Hall.

'Of course—it's my job. I wouldn't be much use to you if I didn't.'

'Forgive me for asking,' she said after a moment's hesitation, 'but have you had much experience? Where have you worked in the past? I know you probably think I should know, but I don't,' she added defensively. 'Obviously my grandmother went into it with you, but I would be glad if you'd tell me.'

'My family have estates in Ireland,' he answered matter-of-factly, without commenting on her remarks. 'I helped to manage them.'

'But why did you leave?'

'My father died.'

'But surely then you would be needed more than ever.'

'My elder brother runs the place now.'

Although his tone did not invite further questioning, Kathryn owned to a certain curiosity as to his background and risked another question. 'How big a place is it?'

'About twice the size of Woollerson,' he answered, leaning forward and switching on the engine. He was looking straight ahead as he spoke and she could read nothing from the expression on his face.

'In that case, I would have thought there would be enough work for both you and your brother,' she ventured as they drove away from the cottage. 'Or perhaps you just wanted a change?'

Zac laughed, but there was no trace of mirth in the sound. 'You could put it like that, I suppose,' he said roughly. 'My brother and I quarrelled and

I decided to leave.' There was a charged silence between them for a few moments, which Kathryn did not dare to break. There was an aura of bitterness about him, a feeling of deep anger which she did not understand but which communicated itself to her, and she was acutely aware that she was at that moment seeing a very different side to the man who was sitting beside her and driving her car but whom she really didn't know at all. 'Now, if you don't mind, Miss Mallory,' he said, breaking the silence with a hard edge to his voice, 'that'll be enough about me. Your grandmother was perfectly satisfied with my credentials and I hope you'll take them on trust. I really don't wish to discuss my private life any further.'

'I really would prefer it if you'd call me Kathryn.' She had blurted out the words almost without thinking and she saw the sudden surprise in his eyes before he laughed. But, although she felt rather foolish, there was no doubt that her words had broken the tension in the atmosphere. 'And I apologise for asking so many questions,' she added hastily. 'I didn't mean to pry.'

'No?' He raised one eyebrow in obvious disbelief but did not pursue the matter. 'So you think I should use your Christian name when addressing you, do you? I wonder if that's a good idea.'

'Why not? It would be ... well, more friendly, wouldn't it?' Stupidly, she felt herself beginning to blush.

'Ah, we're suddenly friends, are we?' Zac grinned at her. 'Calm down, boss, I'm only teasing. Somehow I get the impression that you're not used to being teased.'

Momentarily she frowned, looking for criticism

but finding none. 'Well, I suppose being an only child makes a difference.' Her answer acknowledged the truth of his statement.

'Without a doubt. But, apart from the obvious disadvantages, there are definite advantages to being an only child. Like inheriting this place, for instance.' They were nearly home now and his glance encompassed the lovely sight of a large part of the estate laid out before them. Engrossed as he was in the beauty all about them, he failed to notice the sudden stab of disquiet which momentarily altered Kathryn's expression. Of course it was only to be expected that he would take her inheritance for granted; only she and Mr Barnes knew that it was otherwise. And Brian, she realised with a sudden shock! Then she wondered why on earth this particular aspect of the situation had not occurred to her before. Could she trust him to keep the information to himself, she wondered, or did half the village know as well? Dimly, as if from a great distance, she realised that Zac was saying something and with difficulty brought her thoughts back to the present. 'What's the matter? Have I said something to upset you?' He stopped the car in front of the house and switched off the engine before turning puzzled eyes on her. 'What's up, Kathryn? Don't you fell well?'

She closed her eyes for a minute as all the implications of her new mistrust of Brian were brought home to her, and she groaned aloud before opening her eyes and looking at Zac in sudden desperation. What a fool she'd been to tell Brian so baldly, to leave herself so vulnerable, should he decide to spread the news to all and sundry! All she could hope for now was that he would have the decency to keep it to himself and not make an even bigger fool of her than he had already.

'I'm all right,' she muttered, dragging her gaze away from Zac, determined not to give way to the sudden insane and almost irresistible urge to tell him of her ghastly predicament. She would be much more than a fool if she were to confide in another man. She was badly in need of a friend and confidante, someone to fill the gap left by her beloved Gran, but even to consider that Zac could fill the chasm would, she was sure, be to court disaster. She scrambled quickly out of the car and went into the house, leaving him standing looking after her, a frown between the dark, strongly-marked eyebrows, until eventually he shrugged and walked away in the direction of the stables.

During the next few days Kathryn spent a good deal of her time in the office, sometimes with Zac and sometimes alone, studying maps and plans, going through the accounts and gradually absorbing an enormous amount of information and a mountain of detail relevant to the running of the estate. To her surprise, she found it all fascinating and her enthusiasm for the job grew daily until, as Zac laughingly told her, she was in imminent danger of doing him out of a job.

The atmosphere between them had noticeably improved and no more was said about his leaving. Her respect for him and for his judgment increased enormously and she was soon quite happy to rely on him to make decisions for her. Once she had made up her mind to put her rather childish animosity towards him out of her mind she found that she genuinely liked him, and all formality between them was soon a thing of the past. She was frankly glad of his company and admitted privately that she was sorry when six o'clock came and they closed the door of the office and went their separate ways. Then it was time for Bess's evening walk, and Kathryn was often on the point of asking Zac to accompany them, but she never did, telling herself that he must surely want some time to himself. She knew that he generally drove down to the Red Lion before dinner, but after her first rude refusal he had never asked her to join him.

Her big problem still unsolved, the days slipped past, forming themselves inexorably into weeks, until the time came for Mr Eliot to leave, and soon Zac and Kathryn were immersed in the preparations for his farewell party. She knew that, for a man who had served the estate so well and for so long, her grandmother would have given him a good send-off, and she was determined that this particular party, which was the first one for which she had been responsible, would be at least as good as, if not better than, similar functions in the past.

'Do you think you could run to hiring a group?' Zac asked her one day when they were both in the office discussing the preparations. 'It makes a much better atmosphere than tapes or records.'

'Yes, why not? Good idea. Will you see to it?'

'Of course, if that's what you want.' He sounded surprised. 'But I would have thought that would be more in your line than mine.'

'A couple of years ago it might have been,' she answered, keeping her head down, pretending to be engrossed in the lists of guests which she held in her hand. 'I'm out of touch now.'

'Yes, I've noticed that your social life seems to be pretty well non-existent. No parties, no dances, no boy-friends whizzing up to the house and carrying you off in their fast sports cars. What happened, Kathryn? Somebody let you down?'

'Mind your own business, Zac!' she said rudely, suddenly hating him for hitting the nail so accurately on the head.

'Don't let life pass you by, Kathryn,' he continued as if she hadn't spoken. 'A pretty girl like you should have a string of boy-friends queueing all the way up the drive. Don't let one hard knock ruin your life.'

'Stop behaving as if you were my father!' Suddenly her eyes narrowed and her heart gave a sickening lurch as she looked up at him. 'Have you been listening to gossip in the Red Lion?' she asked sourly. 'I thought better of you.'

'Is there gossip about you in the village?' Zac countered, frowning. 'Because if so, I'll soon deal with it.'

'I've no idea,' she said, suddenly wretched. 'But there could be. Oh, I haven't got an illegitimate child stashed away somewhere, if that's what you're thinking. No, it would be nothing like that.' There was a heavy silence in the small room, eventually broken by Zac.

He perched on the edge of the desk at which she was sitting and looked down at her bent head. 'Who's Brian?' he asked quietly. 'Is he the man who let you down?'

Kathryn swallowed hard before answering. 'You could say so,' she said with difficulty. Then she looked up at him and he frowned at the sudden anguish he saw in her eyes. 'Zac, please tell me what you've heard. I want to know.'

'Very little,' he assured her, 'I promise you. All I gathered was that there was someone called Brian who was generally considered to be your boy-friend, and the consensus of opinion appeared to be that there was a distinct possibility of wedding bells in the near future.'

'And that's all?' she questioned him urgently. 'You promise?'

'That's all.' He answered her seriously because he was aware of her obvious distress.

'Thank God for that!' she exclaimed fervently, suddenly slumping in her chair. 'I don't know what I would have done if. . . .'

'Want to tell me about it?' His blue eyes were fixed on her and he blinked at the vehemence of her reply.

'Good God, no—that's the very last thing I want to do! Oh, sorry, I didn't mean to sound so rude, but you had me worried for a minute.'

'So I perceive,' he drawled. 'Well, if there's nothing I can do, let's get on with this lot, shall we?'

The evening of the party arrived, the small band was in position and Kathryn and Zac met for a quick drink in the drawing room before the first guests began to arrive. The room had been cleared of most of its furniture and the carpets taken up for dancing. It was a very large and elegantly proportioned room and there would be ample space for the two hundred or so people who had been invited. In the dining-room next door a magnificent buffet was laid out and a bar had been set up in the hall.

Kathryn went round quickly turning on every chandelier, wall-light and lamp there was, until the whole of the ground floor was ablaze with light and the air was heavy with the perfume from the armfuls of spring flowers which had been brought in from the gardens and which had taken her virtually the whole day to arrange. Well satisfied with what she saw, she turned to Zac with a smile. 'It really looks beautiful, doesn't it?' she asked, wanting his reassurance.

'Yes, I think we can congratulate ourselves, boss,' he said. 'There's just one thing more. Come over here.' She took his proffered hand and went with him into the hall. Then he stationed her at one of the windows and opened the front door. 'Keep looking down the drive,' he said as he went out, 'and tell me what you think.'

Mystified, she did as she was told, and in a few moments gasped with delight as a multitude of coloured lights sprang into life in the trees on either side of the drive. 'Fairy lights!' she exclaimed. 'Oh, how lovely it looks!' She went to the door and met Zac as he came in.

'Glad you approve,' he grinned at her, and she was suddenly acutely aware of how very handsome he looked in his dinner jacket. 'We used to do it at home sometimes when we were throwing a party.'

She looked at him sharply and did not miss the sudden tightening of the muscles round his mouth. 'I think I can hear a car,' she said quickly, going to stand by the open door. 'They're beginning to arrive. Tell the band to start playing, will you?'

For the next hour Kathryn was kept fully occupied, welcoming the guests, making sure that their glasses were replenished and that they helped themselves to the mountains of food awaiting them in the dining-room. All the maids were on duty and extra staff had been brought in from the village, and Zac appeared to have taken over the running of the bar. Every now and then their eyes met over the heads of the guests and they exchanged a brief smile, a silent acknowledgement that all was going well, before returning to their separate duties.

But when the first rush was over and everyone had arrived, Kathryn went and sat for a moment on a chair behind the bar. 'Now I know what it must be like for the Queen,' she said, flexing the fingers of her right hand. 'It's going well, isn't it?'

'If the noise is anything to go by,' Zac agreed, without turning round, 'I would say it was a smash hit.' He was busy pouring wine into a tray of glasses held by one of the maids. As soon as he had finished and the maid had gone, he deftly opened the next bottle and repeated the performance.

'I must say you make a very good barman,' Kathryn commented.

'Practice, my dear girl,' he grinned at her over his shoulder. 'That's all it takes. Just lots and lots of practice.'

'Did you have lots of parties in Ireland?' she asked, an unconsciously wistful note in her voice.

'Oh, yes, lots. I think the best one I can remember was my coming of age. I got stoned out of my mind but apparently held my drink like a gentleman, or so my father said. They were good days, but it all seems a very long time ago.'

'You look sad, Zac,' she said impulsively. 'I'm sorry—I shouldn't have brought up the subject of

Ireland. You always get that look on your face when you talk about your home.'

'Let's just say that we both have things we'd rather not talk about,' he said, his back to her once more. 'Is Brian here tonight, by the way?'

'No. I didn't ask him.'

'Won't that be commented on?'

'Probably, but that's my business.'

His reply was lost in a sudden crescendo of noise as a bunch of young people erupted into the hall and a very pretty girl whom Kathryn only knew slightly but whose parents had been friends of Gran's descended upon them and seized Zac by the arm. 'Come and dance, Zac darling,' she said as Kathryn's eyes widened. 'You're surely not expected to work all evening!' She gave Kathryn a sidelong glance. 'I really can't let you monopolise the best-looking man for miles around for the whole of the evening!'

'Of course,' Kathryn said brightly. 'I quite agree. You go, Zac. I'll take over, though I'm afraid I haven't had your experience.' Her last words were said to thin air, as Zac was dragged, a girl on each arm, into the swirling mass of dancers in the drawing-room, leaving her momentarily quite alone and suddenly struggling to her disgust and amazement with quite the oddest of sensations. Surely she couldn't possibly be jealous, could she? The idea was absurd, ridiculous, she told herself firmly as she seized the nearest bottle and inexpertly inserted the corkscrew and started to turn. And yet she couldn't quite dismiss the spurt of intense irritation she had felt at the way the girl had commandeered Zac. Not that he had put up much of a fight, she thought sourly. She yanked on the corkscrew and the cork suddenly flew out of the bottle, splashing red wine all down the front of her dress, and for a split second she wanted to scream. 'Damn! Damn! Damn him!' she said under her breath, then called to a passing maid and told her to hold the fort while she went and did something about her dress.

She ran quickly upstairs and into her private bathroom and quickly sponged at the dark red stains on the eau-de-nil silk of her dress, which had been bought specially for the occasion. She had been so pleased when she had found it among the rather limited selection available in Hayersham and she was furious and upset at the thought that it might be ruined, but to her relief she found that her quick action had done the trick and, standing in front of the long mirror in her bedroom a few minutes later, she could see no traces of wine, only large damp patches which were already beginning to dry.

Swishing the long full skirt about in order to accelerate the drying process and still standing in front of the mirror, she thought how lovely the dress was and how well it suited her. One or two of the older men had complimented her on her appearance and she told herself impatiently that she was being very silly when she admitted to being a little hurt that Zac had not. When she had first appeared, dressed and ready to receive her guests, she thought she had detected a gleam of appreciation in his eyes as he looked at her, but he hadn't said a word and she had felt a sharp stab of disappointment at his omission. But then, she quickly reminded herself, complimenting her was definitely not part of his job and he probably wouldn't have cared less if she'd been wearing jeans and a sweater—or even noticed. She turned away from the mirror and, after running a comb through her short blonde hair and adding a touch more lipstick, she quickly left the room and went downstairs to rejoin the party.

She saw at once that Zac had not returned to his place behind the bar and she went to the doorway of the drawing-room and surveyed the crowded dance floor. She pretended that she wasn't looking for anyone in particular, but all the same she was annoyed when there was no sign of Zac. What right had he to leave the bar for so long? she fumed. It was just as well that things seemed to have quietened down in that department. 'Everything all right, Mary?' she asked, walking back to the bar.

'Yes, miss. We were running a bit low on the white, but Mr Wilding's gone to get another case.'

'Oh. Oh, good. That's all right, then.' Kathryn found that she was just as irritated to find that she had misjudged him.

'Why don't you go and enjoy yourself, Miss. I'll stay and help Mr Wilding.'

'Very well,' she agreed hurriedly, feeling suddenly very small and knowing full well the root cause of her pique. 'I think I will.' She went quickly into the drawing-room and almost immediately she was claimed by an old friend of Gran's, a dear old man of whom she was very fond and with whom she dutifully circled the floor a few times before being handed on to old Mr Barnes. Then of course she had to dance with Mr Eliot, who did nothing but sing Zac's praises, which did very little to improve her mood, and he

was followed by old Mr Roberts from the Home
Farm, and so on throughout the evening. It was
not very long before she miserably owned to
herself that she really wasn't enjoying herself at all.
All her dancing partners were so *old* and so *boring*,
and she was soon heartily sick of having to put on
such an act and her face felt stiff with the effort of
maintaining a bright and, she hoped, a not too
obviously false smile.

At one point she did manage to slip away in
order to snatch something to eat, and on her way
through the hall she cast a quick glance over at the
bar and then wished she hadn't, because Zac, or
what little she could see of him, was almost
entirely surrounded by about a dozen of the
prettiest girls, who appeared to be hanging on his
every word. As she passed a wave of laughter in
response to something he'd said assailed her ears
and she gritted her teeth and marched past,
muttering: 'Silly idiots!' under her breath.

To her dismay but not really altogether to her
surprise, there were more old men waiting to
corner her in the dining-room, and when she had
helped herself to some cold turkey and salad, she
resignedly went and sat down among them, only
half listening to them as she wondered acidly why
they weren't dancing with their wives. Then she
remembered the little groups of middle-aged and
old ladies sitting round the edges of the dance
floor and thought that perhaps that was why you
went to a party when you were old, not to enjoy
yourself with your husband but to meet all your
old cronies and have a good gossip, while your
husband was doing the same, preferably in another
room. She knew that she considered the prospect

unutterably dreary and depressing and hoped most fervently that she and her future husband wouldn't end up by being so dull—whoever he might be.

The sudden thought seemed like the very last straw and she looked round desperately, bent on escape, then heard her name being called and looked across the room to find Zac standing in the doorway. 'Miss Mallory, could I have a word?' he called, and when she excused herself and quickly joined him, he added: 'Thought you needed rescuing.'

'Thanks—I most certainly did!' she said with feeling, going with him out into the hall, then couldn't resist adding: 'I would have done the same for you earlier, only you were obviously enjoying yourself. Where have they all gone?' The hall was devoid of pretty girls, she was pleased to see.

'Oh, I sent them packing.' To her ears, he sounded distinctly smug. 'One can have too much of a good thing.'

'I must say, you haven't wasted much time. Where did you meet them all?' She hoped she sounded as if the matter were of purely academic interest to her as she became aware once again that this was not strictly true. Of course she knew everyone who had been invited, but she wondered how Zac had managed to cover so much ground in such a short time.

He shot her a quizzical look from his brilliant blue eyes and there was a hint of laughter lurking round the corners of his mouth. 'Oh, they're the crowd from the Red Lion. They use the place like a club.'

'Oh.' Kathryn knew that deep down in the most

private part of her mind her emotions were oddl
disturbed, and she felt confused and unaccountabl
upset, and to cover up the fact that she couldn'
think of anything to say, she looked at her watch
'Do you think this would be the right time t
make the presentation? It's getting quite late.'

And then quite quickly it was all over. Mr an
Mrs Eliot had left, delighted with their present of
pair of solid silver candlesticks, their eyes a littl
over-bright with the emotion of their leavetaking
the band had packed up their instruments an
gone and the servants were busy clearing away th
debris in the dining-room and hall. Kathryn stoo
in the middle of the dance floor and looked acros
at Zac, who was lounging against the beautiful ol
Adam fireplace, the buttons of his dinner jack
undone and both hands thrust deep into hi
trouser pockets.

'That was a great party,' he said quietl
'Congratulations.'

'You really think it was a success?'

He frowned across at her. 'Of course it wa
They had a whale of a time.'

'Yes, I suppose they did.' Her voice was flat an
she felt unaccountably depressed.

'But you didn't. Is that it?' he questioned he
sharply.

'Of course I did,' she replied a shade to
quickly, and a lopsided smile appeared on his fac

He eased himself into an upright position an
walked casually across the room and bega
turning the knobs on the radio until he found
late-night station which was playing dance musi
'By the way,' he said over his shoulder, '
apologise for not asking you for a dance, but yo

seemed to be more or less permanently in the arms of one old man after another and I never got the chance. However, that is an omission I intend to rectify.' He turned and walked towards her and held out his arms, and Kathryn suddenly found that she had the greatest difficulty in ignoring the eager little shafts of pleasure which shot through her as he clasped her firmly against his chest and they began to dance.

They didn't speak as they glided across the highly polished floor, and she was soon aware that Zac was a very good dancer, making full use of the whole floor which they had so delightfully to themselves. The tempo of the music increased and they adjusted their steps accordingly as if their bodies were moving as one complete entity, and Zac laughed softly and the pressure of his arms about her slim figure strengthened as he crushed her to him, his cheek against hers, the regular beat of his heart thumping out a tattoo of communicated pleasure against her breast. Kathryn's former mood of depression gave way to one of intense enjoyment and she wished they could go on dancing all night. But at last the music stopped and reluctantly she drew away from him a little, but he did not release her immediately and she stood still, strangely unwilling to make the inevitable movement which would break the spell which seemed to have woven itself around them.

'You're a wonderful dancer, Kathryn,' he said at last. 'Thank you. That was the best part of the whole evening.'

'Thank you.' She laughed nervously, absurdly pleased by his words. 'I enjoyed it too.' Then she felt she had to move away from him, because to

stay where she was would have shown him all too
clearly how reluctant she was to go. 'It must be
very late. Time for bed.' And she gave a fair
impression of someone who was really tired out
and ready for sleep. Whereas nothing could have
been further from the truth, for she found herself
all at once completely awake, alert to his every
movement. She could feel his eyes on her and she
pretended to yawn as she turned away from him.
'Goodnight, Zac,' she said quietly. 'Thanks for all
your help this evening.'

'I don't know why I didn't tell you earlier,
Kathryn,' he said quietly from behind her,
completely ignoring her words, 'but you look
stunning tonight. That's a very pretty dress.'

'Compliments from you, Zac,' she said a little
breathlessly as she turned round to face him.
'Whatever next!' The house, she suddenly noticed,
was very quiet and she supposed the servants must
have finished clearing up and gone to bed. Her
eyes met Zac's, which were steadily fixed on her. A
little shiver ran through her and she watched
almost mesmerised as he slowly walked across the
few yards of polished floor that separated them,
knowing what he was going to do and knowing
also that just at that moment it was what she
wanted him to do more than anything else in the
whole world.

And when he took her in his arms and his
mouth came down to find hers, she was quite
unable to summon up even the faintest shred of
resistance to him. Instead she clung to him as her
head whirled and her senses reeled under the
onslaught of his demanding lips. Her past and very
limited experience had not prepared her for

anything like this. Never in her wildest dreams had she imagined that a man could exude so much pent-up passion, such barely controlled force, and she was almost frightened by the certain knowledge that she was completely in his power. His kiss deepened as he forced her lips apart and he crushed her pliant young body so hard against his iron frame that all the breath was forced from her lungs until she dragged her mouth away in order to gain some air. 'Zac, Zac,' she whispered wildly, and then it was she who sought his mouth once more in an ecstasy of abandonment and she exulted in the feel of his steel-like arms clamped immovably round her.

Her hands were inside his jacket and she could feel his warm skin through the thin material of his dress shirt, and as she moved her hands sensually over his body he gave a deep shudder and one of his hands found her small firm breast, while his other hand reached out to find the zip fastening at the back of her dress. Her gasp as she felt the zip running down her back checked his hand and suddenly he froze, holding her without movement for what seemed an eternity, while she felt the passion almost visibly draining out of him. Then he jerked the zip up again and firmly, almost roughly, put her from him. 'I apologise,' he said curtly, meeting her eyes briefly. 'I got carried away. Please forgive me.'

For a moment Kathryn stared back at him, shock and dismay plainly written on her face. She opened her mouth to speak but no words came, then, with a little cry, she turned and ran out of the room. Her legs were shaking and her heart was thumping wildly in her breast as she clumsily negotiated the stairs and reached the safety of her room. Then she threw herself down on to the bed and lay there panting and shivering, moaning wretchedly to herself: 'There's nothing to forgive. Oh, Zac, there's nothing to forgive!'

CHAPTER FOUR

It was a week or so after the party before Kathryn felt completely natural with Zac once more, and in the days immediately following she positively avoided contact with him. His lovemaking had shaken her more than she liked to admit; it had been so totally unlike anything encompassed by her previous experience, forcing an awareness upon her that here was a man, a hard, probably ruthless and passionate male whose instincts in the heat of the moment had got the better of him and she wondered over and over again just how far he would have gone, had he not so abruptly and chillingly come to his senses. Wretchedly, she knew that she was comparing him with Brian and that, without any doubt whatever, the latter paled into insignificance beside him. She also wondered how far she would have wanted him to go, and, in her most honest moments, she knew that she would have been powerless to stop him had he wished to pursue their shared passion to its ultimate conclusion.

Try as she would, she could not get the memory of that night out of her mind, and instead of spending the greater part of her days in the office with Zac as she had grown accustomed to do, she took to going for long walks with Bess, roaming restlessly round the countryside while she strove to regain her old composure. It had been much easier and less complicated, she thought ruefully, when she had felt nothing but wholehearted dislike for her new agent. Everything had been well under control then and she had known exactly where she stood. There had been nothing ambiguous about her emotions in the early stages of their acquaintance: she didn't like him and that was that. Secretly she rather despised herself for altering her opinion of him so quickly, and she wondered whether he for his part basically despised her too.

On one of her long rambles with the now much sleeker and healthier dog, she found herself approaching the cottage which was being renovated for old Mr and Mrs Roberts, and, curious to see how the work was progressing, she approached and, finding the door open, went inside. Sounds of hammering came from the rear and she walked through the sitting-room and into the kitchen, where workmen were busy ripping out rotten floorboards and replacing them with planks of sweet-smelling new wood. It had been decided that the scullery leading off the kitchen was to be converted into a bathroom, and she saw that work was well advanced and the scullery already transformed from a dark and depressing room complete with an old-fashioned copper and a large stone sink, into a light, airy and ultra-modern bathroom. She smiled and, without turning round, spoke to one of the workmen. 'It's a great success, isn't it? I think it all looks lovely.' Then she froze momentarily at the sound of the voice which answered from behind her.

'Surprising what a bit of white paint does to a place, isn't it?' said Zac. 'I was wondering when you were going to put in an appearance.'

'Well, I'm here now,' Kathryn said shortly, smarting under the obvious reproof in his voice, then added: 'I wish you wouldn't creep up on me like that. I didn't hear you come in.' She turned round and scowled at him, partly because he had indeed given her a fright but partly to cover the undeniable pleasure she experienced at the sound of his voice.

'Hardly surprising considering the racket that's going on,' he answered mildly, smiling at her with an amused tolerance. 'Come and look upstairs. It'll be quieter up there.'

She followed him up the narrow staircase and into the larger of the two bedrooms, which on her previous visit had been dark and airless. Now the walls were clad in a pretty rose-covered wallpaper, the paintwork a gleaming white, and the window was wide open, allowing the sound of birdsong and the good country air to fill the room with their joy and fragrance. 'Oh, it's so pretty!' she exclaimed. 'It's perfect! Who chose the wallpaper?'

'I did. I couldn't find you when the men wanted a decision, so I made it for you. I'm glad you approve.'

'I do. You've got good taste. I do hope Mr and Mrs Roberts like it.' Then she walked over to the window and leant out. 'It's so peaceful here, isn't it?' she said, 'when you discount the hammering, that is. I envy them.' She sighed, and Zac laughed from within the room behind her.

'What's this, then? The princess in her castle yearning for the simple life of the peasant in his cottage?'

She ducked back into the room and looked at him crossly. 'Why do you always have to laugh at me! I mean it. I *do* envy them. Their lives are so uncomplicated. They've had a good life at the Home Farm for longer than I can remember, they've had three sons and two daughters and they have I don't know how many grandchildren, and now they have this perfectly sweet cottage in which to spend the rest of their days. It can't be bad!'

'I expect they've had their problems the same as everyone else, Kathryn.'

'Yes, but only little problems, surely?'

'My God, you are a snob!' he laughed. 'I don't suppose they seemed little to them at the time.' There was silence between them as Kathryn walked ahead of him into the smaller back bedroom which had been similarly decorated. 'Do you know how long they've been married?'

'I haven't the faintest idea. Do you?'

'Forty-eight years. You can't tell me they haven't had their share of trouble in all that time.'

'You don't think much of marriage, do you?' she questioned him, suddenly curious. 'Why not? I suppose you're not married, are you?' All at once she wondered why she had assumed that he was unattached and she tried to ignore the sudden coldness which seemed to have descended upon her.

'No.'

She couldn't read anything into his monosyllabic reply, but was aware of a tiny flicker of relief somewhere in the back of her mind. 'Have you been married, then?' She didn't know why she pursued her interrogation, particularly since she saw a glint of anger in his eyes.

'No. I'm not the marrying kind. Not that it's any business of yours, if I may say so.' He turned and walked out of the room and down the stairs ahead of her, and she followed slowly, half regretting being responsible for spoiling the atmosphere between them. She knew she was glad to be talking to him again and resolved to keep off any potentially touchy subjects in future. Then perhaps they could get back to the easy relationship they had had before the night of Mr Eliot's farewell party.

Bidding the workmen goodbye, she walked out into the open to where Bess was lying in the sun, having her tummy tickled by the toe of Zac's shoe.

'She's in much better shape, I'm glad to see,' he remarked, looking up as she approached. 'She's lost a lot of weight.'

'Yes.' Kathryn made a face. 'You were right—as usual.'

'Good of you to admit it.' He grinned at her and she was pleased to see that his good humour was apparently restored. 'Can I give you a lift back?' He indicated the Land Rover parked in the lane.

'Thanks.' She watched as Bess jumped effortlessly into the back of the Land Rover, before getting in beside Zac. 'She couldn't have done that a few weeks ago. She certainly has improved.'

'So have you, boss,' he said with a small chuckle as he started the engine. 'Almost out of all recognition.'

'You've got a nerve!' Although she pretended to be offended, she was pleased at the unexpected warmth in his voice and she relaxed in the seat beside him, all her former embarrassment and perplexity forgotten, happy in the certainty that they were back on their former footing once again.

As they drove through the village, he turned to her. 'Fancy sharing a ploughman's with me at the Red Lion?' he asked.

'I'd love to, but Cook will have lunch waiting,' she answered regretfully.

'Ring her.' He pulled up outside the Red Lion and switched off, then as he saw her indecision, added: 'There's no point in being the boss if you can't do what you want once in a while.' Briefly he put his hand on her shoulder. 'Come on, there's a phone in the bar.'

He jumped down as if it was all settled and she half reluctantly followed him through the low doorway into the sudden gloom of the old inn. Brass and copper winked at her from the walls and the landlord smiled a welcome and suddenly she felt incredibly, almost childishly happy at the unexpected turn of events, and she quickly went to the phone indicated by Zac, as she heard him order a half of lager for her and a pint for himself, two ploughman's and a bowl of water for Bess who, with tongue hanging out, was obediently waiting outside.

Cook having been informed of her change of plan, Kathryn joined Zac at one of the old polished oak tables, and soon she was tucking into the crusty new bread and the large wedge of strong Cheddar, the pungent home-made pickle and the early spring onions, finding herself hungrier than she had been for the past week.

'I did enjoy that,' she said with a satisfied little

sigh when she was back beside Zac in the Land Rover some time later as he drove at a leisurely pace back to Woollerson Hall. 'Not just the food, I mean. Thank you for asking me.'

He turned his head towards her for a moment, giving her an odd look from speculative eyes. 'I must say it doesn't take much to please you—now that we're over phase one, that is.'

'Phase one?'

'When you hated my guts,' he said succinctly. 'You don't now, do you?'

'No, of course not,' she said, looking straight ahead. 'I was in a state and I took it out on the nearest person, who happened to be you. I'm sorry.'

'Apology accepted. Does that mean that you're no longer in a state?'

Kathryn frowned as she shot him a quick glance. 'No, I'm afraid it doesn't. As a matter of fact I'm in a worse state than ever—but I've decided not to take it out on you.' She made a fairly unconvincing attempt at a laugh and her chin went up in the air as if she were daring him to laugh at her.

'Want to tell me about it?' was all he said.

'Oh, no, I couldn't. It's something I've got to work out for myself—though God knows how.'

'O.K., I'll say no more. But the offer stands if you change your mind.'

When they reached the Hall, she went quite naturally into the office with him and they spent the afternoon together dealing with estate business, and, as in the past, the time flew by and for her at least six o'clock came all too soon. As always, when Zac closed the office door behind them, they went their separate ways, but on this particular evening, when Kathryn took Bess down across the lawns for her evening walk, she was sunk deep in thought. The tentative beginnings of a plan were forming themselves in her mind, a plan the very thought of which made her stomach turn somersaults but a plan, nevertheless, which just might work.

During the past ten days' aloofness from Zac when she had gone out of her way to avoid him at all costs, she had even gone to the length of leaving Bess with him overnight. She knew full well that he would look after her and take her for a last run and it meant that she didn't have to go knocking on his door in order to retrieve the dog. However, this evening she intended to revert to the old scheme of things, and accordingly, at about ten o'clock she made her way over to the stables, at first walking briskly and purposefully, but as she approached her pace slackening, because the nearer she got the faster her heart began to beat and the more her legs began to shake, until eventually she came to a full stop at the foot of the short flight of stairs leading up to his door. For several minutes she stood there, torn between a longing to turn tail and flee and a grim determination to carry out her plan. One minute she told herself to forget her crazy and shameless solution to her problem and go back to the safety of the Hall, and the next minute she told herself that if she did that then she was no nearer to finding a way out of her predicament and would have to face up to it sooner or later.

In the end, she took the stairs at a run and knocked desperately at his door as soon as she reached it, giving herself no more time for second thoughts. Her urgency must have communicated itself to him, because the door flew open in record time and he looked at her in alarm. 'Kathryn! What's up?' He took her hand and drew her into the room. 'What's happened?'

'Nothing,' she muttered, immediately feeling incredibly foolish. 'I sort of slipped on the stairs and knocked harder than I meant to. I've only come for Bess.'

'Slipped coming *up* the stairs?' he queried, beginning to smile. 'A bit unusual, wasn't it? Anyway, welcome back, boss. We've missed you, haven't we, girl?' He turned and bent quickly to fondle Bess's ears and Kathryn was relieved that this meant that he looked away from her. 'Sit down,' he added. 'Like a coffee?'

'No ... er ... yes. Oh, I don't know.' She sat down and looked miserably into his puzzled eyes.

'Good lord, you are in a state, aren't you?' he said quietly. 'Hadn't you better tell me what this is all about?'

'That's why I've come. To talk to you, I mean. I've changed my mind. I've got to tell someone, and there isn't anyone else.'

'Thanks!'

'Sorry, I didn't mean it like that. Please don't make it more difficult than it is! And if you laugh at me, I ... I'll throw you out—tonight!' She realised that she was making a complete hash of things and dropped her head into her hands with a groan. 'Oh, God, I didn't mean that either.'

'I promise I won't laugh.' Kathryn took her

hands away from her face and stared hard into his eyes and saw that he was serious. 'Come on, tell me.' His voice was suddenly gentle.

'Zac, I'm in trouble,' she muttered, her head bent.

'You're *what*?' He seized her hands and jerked her half out of her seat. 'You little fool!'

For a moment she gazed at him in amazement, seeing the anger on his face, the look of disgust and impatience. Then she realised what he must be thinking and she started to laugh, more than a little hysterically. 'You didn't think I meant I was pregnant, did you? Oh, Zac, there are more ways than one of being in trouble!' The laughter died within her as he let go of her hands and sat down heavily in the chair opposite hers.

'Thank God for that, at least,' he said, expelling his breath on a loud sigh. 'I didn't think even you could be quite so stupid.'

'*Even* me?' she snapped, stung by the scorn in his voice. 'I thought we'd called a truce. If you're going to be like this, I'm obviously wasting my time. I'll go.' She got up, only to find herself being pushed roughly down again.

'Sit down, girl.' His tone was impatient but not unkind. 'You're very touchy tonight. I apologise if it makes you feel better. Now, will you get to the point?'

With his penetrating blue eyes fixed steadily on her, she felt very foolish and vulnerable and took refuge in continued anger, although it was now partly feigned. 'I came over to talk to you because, as I said, there's no one else. I can assure you that if there was, I wouldn't be bothering you with my worries. What I want to tell you—in fact, what I am going to tell you—is vitally important to me and to Woollerson. And to you too, because if I don't find a solution you'll most probably be out of a job, and time's running out.' She sat forward in her chair and looked at him with agonised eyes, her face beginning to burn, now that the moment had come and she had at last to give life to the words hovering so humiliatingly on her tongue. Zac was staring back at her, deadly serious now, a deep frown creasing his forehead, but he said nothing, thus leaving the way clear for her to continue. 'Believe me, I wouldn't be here now if I wasn't getting desperate,' Kathryn went on wretchedly, 'but it's over two months since my grandmother died, which leaves me. . . .' She gulped and still he said nothing. 'Which leaves me. . . .' she tried again. 'Oh, Zac, I can trust you, can't I?' She knew that by telling him she would be going against her earlier vow never to trust another man, but she also knew instinctively that sitting opposite her was a man of a very different calibre from that of the man who had so badly let her down.

'You know you can,' Zac said now. 'Anything you tell me is safe with me. Go on.'

'Which leaves me,' she repeated, this time finishing with a rush, 'a little under ten months to find a husband!' She met his eyes without flinching and seeing the look of disbelief on his face, rushed on. 'Oh, Zac, I don't even *want* to get married, not yet, but under the terms of Gran's will, if I don't, Woollerson will be sold!'

'Kathryn, you can't be serious! This is ridiculous! Surely you must have got it wrong!'

She saw and sympathised with the look of

incredulity on his face. 'I know it's ridiculous, but I assure you I haven't got it wrong. You can ask Mr Barnes if you don't believe me. He's the only other person who knows...' she paused, then added almost in a whisper, 'apart from Brian.'

'Good God! Now I understand.' Zac's voice was suddenly harsh. 'And the fool turned you down, is that it?' She nodded, and he made a violent sound of disgust. 'You poor kid! Although you must admit it does sound like something out of a romantic novel, I believe you. But it seems a very odd thing for your grandmother to have done, doesn't it? To make such a stipulation? I wouldn't have thought....'

'Mr Barnes said something about making me face up to my responsibilities,' she said bitterly.

'Yes, I see. I suppose she had a point there, but it does seem a bit harsh.' There was silence between them as she watched him assimilate the implications of what she had told him, and when he suddenly returned his gaze to her she knew that he understood completely and was ready for her next words.

'You know what I'm going to say, don't you?' she asked miserably.

'Yes, I think so.' He shook his head quickly. 'Don't say it, Kathryn. It's just not on.'

Feeling suddenly sick and utterly hopeless, she nevertheless relentlessly dragged the words out until they were hanging shamelessly in the air between them. 'As you've obviously guessed, I've come over here tonight to ask you to marry me,' she said tonelessly, her voice quite devoid of expression. 'You said you weren't the marrying kind and I have a feeling I'm not either, so it would be a purely business arrangement. It wouldn't be for any of the reasons why two people usually get married. It would be for Woollerson. I can't let it be sold, and if you don't agree, I'll just have to find someone else. Anyone would do, I suppose. Perhaps I could put an advertisement in the personal column of *The Times*. . . .' Her voice trailed off, because cracks were appearing in the shell of indifference which she had quickly clamped round herself when she saw that Zac was most definitely not interested in her proposal and she had a desperate fear of breaking down in front of him and that, she knew, would be the ultimate humiliation. She stood up abruptly. 'I'm sorry I bothered you,' she said stiffly. 'I'd better go now.' She reached the door and with her hand on the latch looked back at him. 'I hope you won't think too badly of me. I'm really not in the habit of proposing to people, you know.' Then she felt the hot colour flood into her cheeks as she added: 'Well, let's just say that I don't do it very often. Perhaps it'll be third time lucky.' She opened the door as she heard him get up out of his chair and walk across the room towards her. 'Goodnight,' she said quickly, and then she was stumbling down the stairs, her legs shaking as badly as when she had run up them a short while ago.

When she reached the bottom of the short flight, she realised that she had left Bess behind, but she knew that nothing would make her turn and go back for her. She would just have to spend the night with Zac as she had on so many previous occasions, and she knew that the dog would be perfectly all right and that it was she herself who was not perfectly all right.

As she lay in bed some time later, wretchedly going over the scene with Zac, it suddenly occurred to her for the first time that there might have been a particular reason, a very special reason why he had not considered her proposition even for one single moment and that was that he might very well be in love. And the more she thought about it, the more convinced she became that this was indeed the case, and she was startled at the sudden increase in her misery the realisation brought her, as if someone had given a sharp twist to a knife which was already buried deep in her heart.

She wondered what this love of Zac's looked like and who she was. Of course a man as handsome and forceful as he would be attractive to the opposite sex, that was obvious. The only wonder was that he was not married already. Perhaps she was married to someone else and therefore unattainable, but, whatever the truth of the matter, by the time she at last fell into a restless sleep, Kathryn was convinced that the unknown woman was the reason for his leaving Ireland and also for the sadness in his face whenever Ireland was mentioned in conversation between them.

She woke next morning enveloped in a shroud of deep depression. The faint hope that Zac might provide the solution to her problem which had buoyed her up for the past few days was no longer there and, so far as she could see, there was now not even the faintest glimmer of light at the end of the tunnel. Reluctantly she got out of bed and went through the motions of washing and dressing, then went downstairs for a sketchy breakfast. She really didn't feel up to facing Zac this morning and, having eaten as much as she was able to force down, she called to Bess and, after a brief look at the closed door of the office, left the house and set out on one of her marathon walks.

At least Bess seemed to be delighted at the prospect, she noted wryly, and she wished she could summon up from some hitherto untapped resources within herself just a fraction of the enthusiasm displayed by the dog, who was bounding on ahead of her, chasing rabbits both real and imaginary, and dashing back to grin at her mistress every now and then, her tail waving like a golden wand behind her.

But Kathryn, quite unable to catch the infection of joy from the dog, plodded grimly on, enveloped in a fog of depression which was penetrated spasmodically by sharp arrows of panic as she coldbloodedly and systematically ticked off a mental list of all the men of her acquaintance, eligible or otherwise, coming to the conclusion that there was absolutely no one at all who could possibly help her out of her dilemma. Then she remembered her words to Zac of the previous evening, uttered in bitter jest at the time but now giving her fresh food for thought. 'Perhaps I could put an advertisement in the personal column of *The Times*', she had said. Although she knew that she had no intention of doing this, a natural extension of this idea now presented itself to her, and, with the advent of a new plan, her pace quickened and her spirits lifted a little, and she looked about her for the first time and saw that it was a lovely day, the sun was shining, the sky a delicate Dresden blue, and all about her green buds were bursting out of their cold-weather cocoons and thrusting their tender shoots skywards as they basked in the life-giving warmth of the sun.

Bess came hurtling out of the undergrowth towards her and Kathryn laughed to see the dog so happy, bending down and giving her a quick hug when she reached her side. 'There's still a chance, old girl,' she whispered into her silky ear. 'I've got a plan. It's a truly frightful thing to do, but it just might work, and we both think it's worth it, don't we?' Bess licked her face ecstatically before rushing off again and as Kathryn straightened up and slowly followed her, she knew that she intended to leave no stone unturned – no matter what unpalatable prospect she might be forced to contemplate beneath that stone – in order to find herself a husband before the year was up.

Deciding that there was no time like the present, she whistled to Bess and turned and retraced her steps, walking briskly and purposefully back towards the Hall, bent on putting her plan into motion as soon as possible. When she reached the house she went into the library and closed the door firmly behind her, then she collected the morning papers from the table where they were always laid out and sat down to read. She soon found what she was looking for and with an exclamation of satisfaction she took a pen and marked the place with a large cross. Then for the rest of the time before lunch she sat where she was, sunk deep in thought as she mentally composed the letter which she was determined to write that very day.

Emerging from the library a few minutes before one o'clock, Kathryn was embarrassed to see the door to the office open as she walked across the hall. Zac looked up as she passed and their eyes met. She saw that he was frowning as he spoke.

'Where have you been?'

'Out,' she answered briefly, continuing on her way to the dining-room.

She heard him come out into the hall behind her. 'Could you possibly spare a minute – if you're not too frantically busy, that is?' His voice was heavy with sarcasm.

'I'll see you after lunch.' Finding to her disgust that she was shaking and that her heart was bumping uncomfortably against her ribs, she went into the dining-room and closed the door behind her before he could say anything more. She wished she could have avoided him and she was angry with herself for being childish and rude. But really she was angry with him for having the power to knock her off balance, just when she was beginning to recover from last night's fiasco. And the answer to why he was able to knock her off balance, she knew, was that she wished with all her heart that he had been able to accept her bizarre proposition and make it unnecessary for her to pursue her new and even more bizarre line of action. Some instinct told her that she and Zac could have made a successful partnership, even though it would have been a loveless marriage, and as she picked at her food, having suddenly lost her appetite, she became more and more un-enthusiastic about her plan by the minute.

One thing she knew for certain, and that was that she had no intention of seeing him in the

office after lunch, convinced as she was that she
would find it quite impossible to behave naturally
in his presence. Every time she thought about the
previous evening, she became hot with mortification, and her pride dictated that when she did meet
him again, she would have herself under complete
control and that no inkling of her shame and
confusion would be transmitted to him. She
therefore quickly finished her meal and left the
dining-room, then walked quickly and as quietly
as possible over the gravel to the stables where her
car was parked. Presumably Zac would be in his
flat at this hour, but she hoped to get away before
he became aware of her presence. However, when
she arrived at the stables she saw that the Land
Rover was missing and realised that this probably
meant that he wasn't there either. She backed the
car out and drove round to the house to pick up
Bess who loved a ride in the car and would in any
case be company for her. Then she sped away
down the drive, having not the faintest idea of
where she intended to spend the afternoon and not
particularly caring, so long as it was nowhere near
Zac.

She had nearly reached the village when she saw
the Land Rover coming towards her, and she put
her foot down and passed him at speed, head in
the air and eyes looking straight ahead, so that she
wouldn't see the glare which she guessed would be
directed at her. He'd been to the Red Lion, she
supposed acidly, enjoying the company of a gaggle
of silly girls, no doubt. Well, good luck to him, if
that was what he wanted. She really couldn't care
less. His life was his own to do with as he wished,
and never again would she presume to encroach

upon his privacy or seek to alter their respective positions of employer and employee. She wondered if it had been wise to get on a Christian-name footing with him and decided that she would go back to addressing him as Mr Wilding.

She spent an aimless and frustrating afternoon driving around the countryside, occasionally stopping and getting out for a stroll with the dog, then getting back into the car and driving a little further before stopping yet again. The hours crawled by at a snail's pace and even stopping for tea in Haversham only took up half an hour, but she was determined to delay her return until after six o'clock when she had every reason to suppose that Zac would be out of the way. She felt very silly and frankly admitted that her behaviour was decidedly juvenile, but she knew that she had to keep out of his way for the time being and was sure that, had she stayed in the house, he would have succeeded in tracking her down had it suited his purpose.

At last she deemed it safe to return, and she turned the car and headed for home. Although Bess wouldn't really need her six o'clock walk, it would soon be time to feed her and it wasn't fair to keep her out any longer. As she approached the house and not really to her surprise she saw the Land Rover coming towards her again. Really, the man must be quite a drunkard, she thought nastily as she sped past him without any intention of meeting his eyes. Then at the last moment something impelled her to cast a quick glance in his direction and she saw that he was openly laughing at her as he raised his hand in a brief salute before the vehicles were past one another.

What the Red Lion had done without his custom in the past she couldn't imagine, she told herself pettishly as she drove on, but then he must have money to burn, since his salary was a generous one and he also had an aura about him which suggested that he was probably quite wealthy in his own right. Which, she acknowledged with a sudden straightening of the normally soft curve of her lips, was one of the reasons why he would have been a good choice as a husband, being quite clearly no fortune-hunter.

Later that evening, after dinner, Kathryn went into the library once more, determined on writing the letter which she had been mulling over in her mind during most of the afternoon and evening. First she read again the item in the paper which she had marked with a cross earlier in the day, then, with a decidedly grim expression on her face, took a sheet of writing paper from the desk and began to write. It was arguably the most difficult letter she had ever had to write, and she was completely engrossed in her task, otherwise she might have been aware that someone was approaching the library door, before it was abruptly opened and Zac strode into the room. Startled, she looked up and, when she saw who it was, quickly covered the sheet of paper in front of her with both hands.

'What are you doing here?' she asked ungraciously, wishing her heart would do something about its maddening and extremely disturbing habit of beating at twice its normal rate whenever she came across him unexpectedly.

'I want to talk to you,' he replied, apparently

quite unperturbed by her unfriendly greeting. 'Mary said I'd find you in here.'

'Oh, she did, did she? I'll have to speak to her about that.' Kathryn got up from her place at the desk and moved away, hoping that this would take his attention away from what she had been doing, had he noticed that she had something to hide. But she might have known that he would not be so easily distracted, and with dismay she saw his eyes go straight to the sheet of paper, now no longer hidden, lying in full view on the desk.

'Writing letters, are you?' he asked pleasantly enough. 'Sorry to disturb you, but it's rather important. Oh, is that today's paper? Do you mind?' And before she could do anything to stop him he had picked up the paper and was quite openly reading the advertisement which she had marked. She saw him suddenly become very still and she felt a strong and urgent desire for the floor to collapse beneath her feet and take her immediately from his view. 'If you don't want people to know what you're up to, it's very silly to put a bloody great cross where anyone can see it, don't you think?' His voice was very low as he turned and looked at her, and Kathryn jumped and gave a small cry when he suddenly hurled the paper straight at her. Automatically, she put out her hands and caught it, then she dropped it as she defiantly stared back at him. She could see that he was very angry, but then so was she.

'It's none of your damn business!' she said furiously. 'How dare you come barging in here like this. Kindly get out—Mr Wilding!'

'Oh, dear, we're back to square one, are we?' he said with an impatient sigh. 'It really is time you grew up, you silly little girl. And as for this . . .' Suddenly he swooped down at her feet and, picking up the paper waved it contemptuously in her face. 'You must be out of your mind! A marriage bureau! Girls like you do *not* go to places like that!'

'For God's sake!' she yelled back at him. 'What else can I do? You *know* I'm desperate, so what the hell am I supposed to do? If you're so damn clever, you tell me! Go on, tell me!'

Suddenly the anger seemed to drain out of him and he gave her a lopsided grin. 'That's precisely what I came to do, boss,' he said surprisingly gently. 'In fact it's what I've been trying to tell you all day, but you will keep avoiding me. If you'd only stood still long enough for me to catch up with you just once today, it would have saved us both a lot of trouble.'

She wrinkled her brow, still angry and confused but taking her cue from his tone. 'What do you mean? I don't understand.'

'I've changed my mind.'

Her heart gave a sickening lurch but, not daring to hope, she persisted, 'I still don't understand.'

'Oh, yes, you do. That's something we'll have to get straight before we go any further. Don't ever lie to me. I can read you like a book.' Zac kept his eyes fixed on hers as he took a couple of steps towards her. 'But if it'll make you feel better, I'll spell it out for you. I've decided to accept your proposition.' Before she could speak he turned and walked over to the desk and picking up her letter he tore it into little pieces and dropped them into the wastepaper basket. 'So you won't be needing that, will you?'

'But why?' To her own ears her voice sounded odd. 'Why, have you changed your mind?'

'I did a lot of thinking last night after you'd gone, and by dawn's early light I'd come to the conclusion that it might not be such a bad idea after all. I think it just might work—once I've tamed you. O.K., don't blow your top, that was a joke—more or less. But if we're going ahead with this, let's get one thing straight from the start. I'll be the boss. Oh, of course, I don't mean so far as the estate is concerned, I'm referring to our proposed alliance. No wife of mine will ever tell me what to do—ever. Is that understood?'

Since he was evidently waiting for an answer, Kathryn nodded, albeit rather briefly. She was determined that Zac should not see how unutterably relieved she was and that so far as possible he should not be left too obviously with the impression that he was doing her a favour, although of course they both knew full well that he most certainly was.

'In the comparatively short time I've been here I've grown to love this place,' he went on seriously, 'and I agree it would be a crime to let it go. So shall we say we're both doing it for Woollerson? That'll make you feel better about it, won't it?'

'Yes,' she answered clearing her throat, feeling suddenly ill at ease with him now that it had been decided that their relationship was going to change so drastically. 'But of course you do understand that it's purely a business arrangement, don't you?'

She felt her cheeks begin to burn as she saw him smile. 'I mean, it won't be a marriage in the ordinary sense of the word.'

'You mean no sex,' he said, his voice deadpan but the smile still hovering round his lips. 'Of course, my dear. I'm sure we would both find that most distasteful wouldn't we?'

CHAPTER FIVE

WHEN she woke next morning, for a few moments Kathryn could not understand why she felt so good. She was aware that she had slept better than for many a long night, but this alone could not account for the unaccustomed sensation of wellbeing which spread over the whole length of her body as she stretched in a leisurely fashion before getting out of bed. Then suddenly she came fully awake as she remembered the real reason, and she paused in the act of throwing back the covers as something inside her gave a great leap and a tide of happiness and relief flooded over her. 'Thank God!' she said aloud, sitting up in bed and hugging herself. 'It's all going to work out after all.'

She sang as she quickly showered and dressed and as she left her room she executed a little dance on the landing before making for the stairs, leaping down them two at a time as she hadn't done since she was a child in a sudden exuberance of youth and vitality. In mid-flight she became aware that, of all people, Zac had to be standing in the hall watching her, but she was going too fast to stop and she landed more or less at his feet, slightly out of breath and with cheeks aglow from the unaccustomed exercise.

'Well, good morning.' She looked up and saw the glint of laughter in the blue eyes regarding her. 'You seem in high spirits today.'

'Well,' she suddenly grinned up at him, 'it's a lovely day, isn't it? Why shouldn't I be in high spirits?' She was in the act of turning in the direction of the dining-room and a breakfast for which she was all at once ravenously hungry, when she gave him a second glance. 'What's all this, then?' She looked him up and down, then slowly circled round him, taking in the well-cut suit, expensive-looking shirt and silk tie. His clothes were in startling contrast to his usual wear of old cords and a sweater worn over an open-necked shirt, or even jeans if a visit to one of the farms was on his schedule for the day. 'To what do we owe this honour? Mind you, I'm not complaining. You look terrific, but what's it all in aid of?'

With an exaggerated sigh he took hold of her arm. 'Would you mind, you're making me giddy. Stop walking round me as if I'm an exhibit in the zoo, would you? We are going to London, fiancée mine, to buy you a ring. So don't take too long over breakfast.'

'Oh!' Taken completely by surprise, it was all Kathryn could think of to say. 'Are we?' Then she looked down at her denim skirt and cotton blouse. 'Then I'll have to change, won't I?'

'It would be appreciated.'

'But why London? There's a perfectly good

jewellers in Haversham. And anyway, you don't have to buy me a ring.' She looked up at him, a half smile attempting to conceal her embarrassment. 'It doesn't really seem right somehow. I mean, why should you?'

'Nonsense,' he said impatiently. 'Of course you must have a ring. And if we're going through with this, we're going to do it in style. So I repeat, we're going to London.' His last words were said on a lower note and for her ears only, and he stood looking at her for a moment in silence with one eyebrow slightly raised. Then he smiled briefly and turned to go back into the office. 'Get a move on—I thought we'd catch the ten o'clock train.'

Thus dismissed, Kathryn went quickly into the dining-room and hastily drank a glass of orange juice, then buttered a piece of toast and poured herself a cup of coffee. She was suddenly happy at the thought of a day out, and she would in any case have been less than human if she had not been excited by the prospect of being taken to London to buy her engagement ring. The thought of a ring hadn't entered her head, but now that it had been put there by Zac, she realised that he was right and that it would doubtless be thought very odd indeed if she did not have one. She finished her coffee and poured herself another cup, her mind now fully occupied with deciding what she was going to wear. She had to leave half her second cup because it was too hot and she was going to need all the time she had at her disposal if she was not to let Zac down on their first outing together. She quickly left the dining-room and ran upstairs.

Once in her bedroom she went to the wardrobe and took out a lightweight pale grey flannel suit, a cream silk blouse and brown court shoes, then from a drawer she took a brown leather handbag and gloves. It took her very little time to change and she stood for a minute surveying herself critically in the long mirror, then took a large cameo brooch in a heavy gold setting and pinned it to her lapel and stood back with a satisfied smile. 'Find fault if you dare, Zac,' she said quietly, knowing that she looked good, then, picking up her bag and gloves, she left the room and went quickly downstairs.

Zac came out of the office looking at his watch. 'Well done,' he said, casting a brief glance in her direction. 'We should make it all right.' He held the front door open for her and she walked past him and out into the open, impatiently dismissing a small stab of disappointment at his complete lack of comment on her appearance. 'I thought we'd take your car,' he said, joining her. 'It's cleaner than the Land Rover. In you get.'

The journey to London was uneventful and Kathryn spent the time staring out of the window while Zac buried himself behind *The Times*. At the station he had asked her if she would like a paper, but she had refused, knowing that she wouldn't have been able to concentrate. Her earlier feeling of excitement was quickly evaporating in the face of his indifference, and she had to keep reminding herself that he was perfectly justified in his attitude and that they were simply carrying out the first stage of their coldblooded arrangement, in which there was clearly no place whatever for emotion of any sort. However, she sighed deeply once or twice and on each occasion felt his eyes rest briefly on her before returning to his paper.

When they reached Liverpool Street, Zac hailed a taxi which took them straight to Bond Street, and when they pulled up outside the opulent exterior of a world-famous jewellers, she drew in her breath sharply and looked at him in amazement. 'We're not going in there, are we?' she asked, thinking it had probably merely been the most convenient place for the driver to stop.

'Of course.' There was a gleam of humour in his eyes as he handed her out and paid the cabby. 'I said we'd do it in style, remember? Come on, in you go!'

The discreet uniform of the doorman as he held the door open for them, the deep pile of the dark blue carpet once they were inside, the frock-coated man gliding silently and immediately towards them, the muted sounds and the soft lights, all went to create an atmosphere of great and unhurried wealth. The counters, if such they could be called, lay in isolated pools of light, a large expanse of carpet between each affording complete privacy for every customer, and Kathryn automatically straightened her shoulders and held her head high as they were led to their own particular spotlighted island, as if a visit to such a place were quite a commonplace occurrence and certainly did not overawe her in the least.

Trays of rings were brought for her inspection and when the assistant left them for a moment to fetch more, she whispered to Zac: 'They must all be terribly expensive. Don't you think we ought to go somewhere else?'

'Oh, dear, don't you see anything you like?' he asked, deliberately ignoring her actual words. 'Perhaps he's bringing one which will appeal to you.'

'They're all fabulous, absolutely beautiful,' she answered, keeping her voice low. 'But I'm embarrassed. I don't want you to spend so much on me—it isn't right.'

'Allow me to be the judge of that,' he returned evenly, but the look in his eyes as they briefly met hers quelled any further protest from her. 'My fiancée is having a little difficulty in making up her mind,' he said, turning with a smile to the returning assistant. 'Perhaps you have something there. What do you think, darling?' He took a ring from the new tray and slipped it on her finger, holding her hand in his as they gazed at the ring together. For the life of her, Kathryn couldn't have said a word just at that moment. The unexpected endearment, although of course completely false, had momentarily thrown her off balance, and she stared dumbly at the diamonds and sapphires flashing and shining up at her from a hand which suddenly looked very small and white as it rested in the firm grasp of the man who she had the greatest difficulty in thinking of as her future husband.

'It's beautiful,' she said at last, her voice a little breathless. 'Really lovely. I . . . I'd like this one, please.'

'Of course, darling, if you're quite sure.'

She nodded. 'Yes, I'm sure.' However, she wished Zac would stop calling her that.

'Right, that's settled.' He let go of her hand, and she took off the ring and placed it carefully on the black velvet-covered board which the assistant had placed on the counter. 'Why don't you keep it on?' he added, as he reached into an inner pocket for his cheque book.

But Kathryn shook her head. 'No, I'd rather not.' She saw that the assistant was putting the ring into a little leather box. 'You keep it for the moment, will you?'

He gave her a puzzled look. 'Very well, if that's what you want. Now go for a little walk round, will you, darling, while I settle the sordid details.'

Glad to move away from him, she drew a deep breath and went and stared with unseeing eyes at a glass case full of Georgian silver, but she was in no mood to appreciate the beauty before her. Stupid tears were burning her eyes and she was mentally desperately searching for distraction until she could compose herself sufficiently to make it possible to turn round and face Zac once more. She knew perfectly well why she was feeling so wretched, and she cursed herself impatiently for being such a fool, telling herself angrily that she should count herself lucky to have found herself such a presentable husband, and well within the stipulated time too, and that she must be a complete idiot if she expected for one single instant that she could ever have hoped to have found romance as well. The choosing of the engagement ring was simply part of the transaction and had nothing whatever to do with the normal feelings of a conventional bride-to-be. Those feelings had had to be sacrificed on the altar of the all-important and much-loved Woollerson, and the sooner she came to terms once and for all with the facts of her life now and in the foreseeable future the better. It was absolutely pathetic and utterly pointless to cry for the moon as well.

Once outside and with the magnificent ring safely in Zac's pocket, she withdrew her hand from where he had tucked it under his arm as they left the jewellers. She felt an urgent need to get away from him, and when he asked her what she would like to do, since it was a little early for lunch, she said almost the first thing which came into her head. 'There's something I've always wanted to do,' she said, assuming a falsely bright and cheerful air, 'and that's have my hair done in a famous London salon. Would you mind?'

'Typical woman!' he laughed. 'No, of course I wouldn't mind. Where do you want to go?'

'I don't know exactly, but I'll know it when I see it. Let's go down here.' They turned left into Albemarle Street and almost immediately Kathryn found what she was looking for and looked up at him enquiringly. 'Can I go in and see if they can fit me in?'

'Of course, darling. You don't have to ask my permission. I don't own you, you know, even if I have just bought you an incredibly expensive engagement ring.' Although he was smiling, his words cast a chill over her just when she was beginning to recover her composure, and her mouth tightened as she looked at him from smouldering eyes.

'I told you not to waste your money on me.' she snapped, 'so don't go throwing it in my face now. And cut out this "darling" nonsense, will you?— It's ridiculous. I'll see you later.'

She reached out for the door of the salon, but

Zac seized her arm and pulled her back, holding her briefly and uncomfortably against him. 'I can assure you that I do not consider that I've wasted my money, as you so charmingly put it, Kathryn,' he said quietly. 'It's really a matter of pride—mine, not yours. I'm not having my wife wearing anything that looks cheap. And once again you've demonstrated that your sense of humour rapidly deserts you when you are being teased. Don't be so touchy in future, or you're going to make life quite impossible.' She struggled to get free of him without making it too obvious to passers-by that he was holding her against her will, and he relaxed his grip but still held her arm. 'Now,' he said, giving her arm a little jerk, 'go and get your hair done. I expect you'll find someone who can do it, even if they can't here. We'll meet for lunch at one-thirty. There's a place I know in Soho called Emilio's. You'd better take a taxi or you'll get lost.' Then to her utter amazement, particularly in view of the curtness of his tone, he swiftly bent his head and kissed her very firmly, almost unpleasantly, on the lips, thus depriving her of the breath she needed to form the words she had intended to use in a biting retort. 'Au revoir, my beloved fiancée,' he said, holding open the door of the salon for her. 'Have fun!'

It was some time before Kathryn calmed down enough to enjoy the ministrations of the experts in whose hands she found herself, but eventually she succumbed to the soothing effect their efforts produced and realised that her spur-of-the-moment idea had been truly inspired and that probably nothing else could have been guaranteed to restore her spirits and boost her ego to such an extent. Although she had worn her pretty fair hair quite short for several years, the style which she saw being created for her now went much further than she would normally have dared, but in the mood in which she had entered the salon she had felt that she didn't really give a damn what they did to her and so had given the stylist a free hand. 'You have pretty ears,' he had said, walking slowly round her and viewing her face from every angle, 'so why not show them? May I?'

She nodded. 'Go ahead. I leave it to you.' And she watched closely as the scissors began to fly, only admitting to an occasional stab of anxiety as her hair began to fall to the floor. But she soon relaxed under the obvious expertise of his clever hands and eventually emerged into the street once more, excited and elated by her changed appearance. She looked at her watch and saw that it was already after one-thirty, but she did not let this upset her unduly as she walked down the street in search of a taxi, casting constant glances at herself in shop windows as she passed. He'd just have to wait, she told herself. She couldn't help wondering what his reaction would be when he saw her—not that his opinion mattered to her one way or the other, of course, but she wondered all the same.

She found a taxi and ten minutes later it deposited her outside the little restaurant in Greek Street, and she paid the driver and went inside. Although the place was crowded she spotted Zac almost immediately and saw him get to his feet, pointedly looking at his watch. The lighting was subdued and for a moment she felt sure that he hadn't noticed her appearance, but as she advanced towards him she saw his jaw drop in an almost comical fashion and her head went up in the air as it always did when she was not too sure of herself, until she reached his side. 'Good grief?' he exclaimed. 'What a transformation! Turn round—slowly.' Quite unable to gauge his reaction from his expression or his tone of voice, Kathryn did as he said, noting as she did so the amused glances of the people sitting at adjacent tables, then she sat down quickly in the chair which he was holding out for her.

A waiter approached and handed her the menu, and she dropped her eyes gratefully, pretending to be quite unaware that she had made any particular impression on Zac one way or the other. 'Have you ordered?' she asked with masterly sangfroid. 'I'm sorry I'm late, by the way.'

'No, I haven't, and it's quite all right.' His voice sounded different somehow and she looked up in surprise, to find him staring at her with a strange and unfamiliar expression on his face. 'Absolutely stunning! You look fantastic!'

Now it was the turn of Kathryn's jaw to drop. 'Do you really mean that? You like it?' In spite of herself, she was quite unable to prevent a smile from slowly lighting up her face.

'My God!' he said slowly. 'I always thought . . . But this is something else! You're beautiful!' His eyes narrowed, then he cleared his throat and gave himself an almost invisible shake. 'They evidently make a very good job of turning sows'. ears into silk purses at that famous salon of yours.' He grinned, and she was relieved to see that the familiar Zac had reappeared. 'Now will you kindly turn your attention to the menu and be quick about it. I'm starving!'

The atmosphere between them was relaxed and friendly as they tucked into the excellent food, and throughout the meal Kathryn was aware of a sensation of warmth within her brought about by Zac's unexpectedly wholehearted admiration of her new hairstyle and the increase in self-confidence that this brought her. And it was not until they had reached the coffee stage that he threw her off balance again by taking the small box from his pocket and placing it on the table in front of her. 'Why didn't you want to wear it earlier?' he asked as she stared awkwardly down at the tiny box.

'I really don't know,' she answered quickly. 'I was just being stupid, I suppose.'

'No, there *was* something going on in that beautiful head of yours,' he persisted. 'I want to know what it was.'

'Really, Zac, it was nothing,' she assured him impatiently. 'Please don't embarrass me here in front of all these people.' Quickly she reached out and opened the box, then drew her breath in sharply as the sheer beauty of the ring hit her. On its own and away from all the other rings in the jewellers it looked even more beautiful than she had remembered, and she gazed at it, finding it difficult to believe it was really hers.

Suddenly Zac's hand came out and he took the ring from its box. 'As a matter of fact I think I can guess what you were thinking,' he said. 'Give me your hand. Is that better?' And he slipped the exquisite circlet on to the third finger of her left hand, while she watched, completely at a loss for words, and they were both startled when the waiter spoke from behind them.

'Champagne, sir?'

Zac looked at him for a moment, then grinned. 'Why not? Moët-Chandon, please.' Then he looked at Kathryn and they stared at one another, her hand in his, as the waiter glided quietly away. The expression on Zac's face was completely serious as he continued to hold her hand and she felt sure that he was on the point of saying something, something important, when the waiter reappeared in record time and the moment passed.

Filled with good food and having drunk more champagne than was probably wise, Kathryn dozed in the train going back and had to be roused by Zac shaking her when they reached their station, and she was glad when he took her arm and propelled her out of the station to where they had left the car. He drove quickly home while she lay back in the seat beside him, yawning prodigiously and more than half asleep, and when they reached the house, he took her arm again and helped her indoors. 'I'm afraid I drank a bit too much champagne,' she observed, looking at him through eyes which wouldn't quite focus.

'Yes. I should go and lie down if I were you. I'll see you in the morning.' His tone was matter-of-fact, almost brusque, and he abruptly left her, standing in the middle of the hall and gazing at the front door which had already closed behind him.

'In the morning?' she repeated, frowning, 'but I thought. . . .' All at once the lovely warm, blurred feeling which had enveloped her and made her feel so happy began to disappear, to be replaced by a cold and wretched misery which was so sudden and so intense that she shivered and then hugged herself convulsively in an urgent search for warmth. He certainly had a finely developed talent for bringing her down to earth, she thought bitterly as she moved towards the stairs and it was little comfort to her when she reminded herself for about the tenth time that day that Zac was under no obligation whatever to dance attendance on her at any time and that he had been quite unnecessarily generous already. No, she told herself dejectedly as she wearily climbed the stairs, she did not expect or even want him to pretend to entertain feelings for her which could only be feigned, and it was totally unreasonable of her to want him to spend any more of his time with her that day, so it must therefore surely be the champagne which was making her feel so unreasonably and suddenly deflated.

It was a few days later when Zac broached the subject of the wedding itself. 'I take it that, under the circumstances, the nearest registrar's office will do?' They were together in the close confines of the office and he could not fail to notice her stricken look as her head jerked up and their eyes met. 'Oh, dear,' he sighed impatiently, 'I see it won't.'

'I'm sorry,' Kathryn muttered in confusion, looking away quickly. 'Yes, of course that would be the sensible thing to do.' But she couldn't quite keep the disappointment out of her voice and he rested his hand briefly on her shoulder.

'But you obviously don't feel like being sensible, do you?' There was a long silence, then he sighed again. 'I suppose it would be pretty rotten to deprive you of what's supposed to be the most important day in a girl's life. I imagine you want the whole works?'

'Well, I think the village and the estate workers would expect it,' she parried, keeping her face averted.

'Oh, yes, of course.' The sarcasm in his voice was only just detectable. 'But it's hardly appropriate, would you think?'

'In a position like mine,' she said, suddenly raising her head and looking at him defiantly, 'one can't always do what one wants—as my grandmother often said. People might think I'm pregnant or something if we creep off and do it in a hole-and-corner fashion.'

'Of course, why didn't I think of that? How inconsiderate of me! But hasn't it occurred to you that they may think that in any case? It's all been a bit sudden, hasn't it?'

She closed her eyes for a moment as the full implication of his words hit her. 'Then we'd better postpone it until the last possible moment,' she said at length. 'Then there can be no doubt in anyone's mind.' All at once she found she felt slightly sick.

'No,' Zac said firmly, 'we'll stick to the date we've decided on. After all, if anyone does have any thoughts along those lines, they'll soon be proved wrong, won't they?'

'Yes.' She swallowed, studiously avoiding his gaze, and another long silence ensued.

'Well, boss,' he said at length, 'if it's to be a white wedding, hadn't you better be doing something about buying a dress?'

'You mean you don't mind?'

'I don't mean anything of the sort. I mean I'm willing to put up with it if it really means so much to you, that's all. I suppose I've got to wear a morning suit?'

'Yes, please.' Suddenly she looked up at him and grinned. 'You know you'll look fantastic, so what are you moaning about?' The atmosphere in the small office had noticeably lightened and she felt able to tease him.

'Of course I shall. I only hope you can live up to it. You'll keep your hair the way it is, won't you?'

'Yes.' She smiled as she bent her head over the accounts she'd been looking at before he had started the conversation. 'I'll go up to London and get it done the day before.' A warm glow of happiness was creeping over her, a sensation which she had recently discovered could only be induced by the actions or words of the man who was so frighteningly soon to be her husband, and although past experience told her that it wouldn't last, it was very good while it did. On rare occasions, and only since they had been to London to buy the ring, she thought she had detected the first fragile beginnings of a bond between them, and when she was feeling at her most optimistic she thought there might be a real hope of happiness for them in the future. Arranged marriages had been known to work out very well and to last, when those entered into by two people trapped in the false and over-idealistic web of romantic love often foundered. 'I think I'll go to Harrods for my wedding dress,' she added dreamily, and stared out of the window, her mind completely taken up with such things as materials.

necklines, length of sleeves and headdresses, so that she was unaware of the odd expression on Zac's face as he looked down at her.

'There's something else we must do if we're going to have a church wedding,' he said brusquely, 'and that is go and see the vicar. I hope you realise you're going to have to promise to obey me.'

'What?' She came back to earth with a jolt. 'You must be joking! The bride doesn't have to promise anything so ridiculous nowadays. Times have changed, thank goodness.'

'Oh, well, if you're not prepared to promise that, the deal's off.'

'Don't be silly, Zac! You are joking, aren't you?' She looked at him, almost sure that he was teasing, but his expression gave nothing away. 'I remember what you said about being the boss, but you wouldn't really expect me to promise anything so outlandish, would you? I don't like the idea of making a solemn promise in church which I have no intention whatever of keeping.'

Zac looked down at her and his expression was grim, though she still couldn't tell whether it genuinely mirrored his feelings. 'Why don't we take a look at the marriage service in the prayer book and see just what it says?'

'I'll get mine. It's in my room.' Kathryn stood up and moved towards the door. 'But it's one I've had for years and of course it will say I have to promise to obey.'

'I realise that, but there are other promises we shall have to make. Don't you think we'd better find out just what is entailed?'

In a few minutes she returned to the office with

the open prayer book in her hand, having quickly read through the marriage service in the privacy of her bedroom, and she handed it to him wordlessly and went and stared out of the window. Stupidly, the words 'love, honour and keep him in sickness and in health; and, forsaking all other, keep thee only unto him so long as ye both shall live' had brought a lump to her throat, and she wanted a moment to compose herself. Much later she was to wonder whether that was the moment when she first realised that she might be falling in love with him. She wondered what was going through his mind as she heard him turn the fragile leaves of the book which had belonged to her mother. If he were to scoff or make fun in any way whatsoever, she swore she would call the whole thing off there and then.

But there was no hint of mockery in his voice when he spoke. 'We'll forget about the "obey" bit if it bothers you.' She heard him close her prayer book and put it down on the desk. 'And as for the rest—well, we're going to try and make this thing work, aren't we, so I don't think it would be too hypocritical to go along with it, do you? Look at me, Kathryn—this is fairly important, you know.'

She turned round and faced him then. 'I know it is.' Her voice was not much more than a whisper and she found she was twisting her engagement ring round and round on her finger. 'If you want to back out, now's the time to do it.'

Zac frowned. 'Whatever made you think I wanted to back out?'

She shrugged. 'I don't know, really. I just

thought perhaps. . . .'

'Well, you can stop thinking. We're going ahead and that's that.' He glared at her for a moment, then picked up the telephone. 'Find me the vicar's number and I'll give the old boy a ring at once.'

The weeks flew by, and Kathryn experienced an increasing sensation of panic as the first Saturday in September rapidly approached. Fortunately she had a great deal to do and every waking moment was fully occupied with the preparations, but this did not prevent her from thinking, and at night she had to make a conscious effort to switch off and try to make her mind a complete blank, otherwise she felt sure she wouldn't have been able to sleep at all. Since they had become engaged she had become aware of an increasing liking and respect for this comparative stranger to whom she was so soon to be bound by the state of matrimony. That he knew his job had been apparent from the very beginning, and she soon learnt not to question any decision he made. He was also clearly popular with the tenants and estate workers, and indeed with everyone he met, both as the estate's agent and as her fiancé, and Kathryn herself was soon perfectly ready to admit that he could be very good company indeed. But she could not fail to notice that he seemed to become increasingly preoccupied as their wedding day approached, and she felt less able to talk to him naturally as time went by, until she was forced to wonder whether, in spite of what he had said in the past, he was now regretting his acceptance of her extraordinary proposal, and these thoughts led her inevitably to considering once again the possibility that he might be in love with someone else, a woman whom he had, for some reason beyond her understanding, left behind in Ireland.

A party of about twenty of his friends were coming over for the wedding, but he had made it very clear that his brother and sister-in-law were not to be invited, and although Kathryn felt it was extraordinary and quite wrong that the only family he had would not be present, the expression on his face when he had told her of his decision had made it quite impossible for her to argue, and she had reminded herself that it was in any case entirely his affair and no concern of hers. Her guest list was ten times the length of his, consisting of more or less the same people as had been invited to Mr Eliot's farewell party, and it had therefore been decided to mix all the guests together so that the pews on one side of the church were not bursting to overflowing, while those on the other were only sparsely filled. Mr Barnes was to give her away, and since she had no close girl friends in the neighbourhood, two old school friends had been contacted and, although somewhat surprised, had seemed happy to accept her invitation to act as her bridesmaids.

It was a bare two weeks before the wedding, the preparations were complete, her beautiful dress from Harrods was hanging under its covers in her wardrobe, the flowers had been ordered, the food and drink organised, and all that remained for Kathryn to do was to sit back and pray for a fine day—when Mr Barnes dropped his bombshell. He came to see her by appointment and about a matter which he said could not be discussed over the telephone. As she put the receiver down after his call, she wondered with a vague feeling of unease whether what he had to tell her could have anything to do with the wedding, but nothing in her wildest imaginings could have prepared her for the shock which was awaiting her and which was contained in the form of a letter from her grandmother which Mr Barnes handed her when he called on her the following day.

'Following your grandmother's instructions,' he said in his usual rather pompous fashion, 'I have to hand you this letter two weeks before your wedding day.'

'A letter from Gran?' Kathryn questioned, completely mystified. 'I hope it's not bad news. I can do without that just now, with the wedding and everything . . .'

'I have no way of telling whether you'll consider it good news or bad, my dear,' he said on a sigh. 'Kindly read it.'

With a slightly sick feeling in the pit of her stomach and suddenly remembering how she'd felt on being acquainted with the extraordinary terms of Gran's will, Kathryn slowly slit open the envelope and taking out the single sheet of paper, began to read. 'My dear child,' she saw written in Gran's forceful handwriting, 'If you are reading this, then it is because you have acceded to my wish that you settle down and manage Woollerson Hall and the estate and are to be married in two weeks' time. The terms of my will may have distressed you and made you angry, but believe me, I had only your best interests at heart. I think you will realise that this is true when I tell you now that, as you have faced up to your responsibilities as I knew you would, I here and now release you from the terms of my will. If in order to keep Woollerson you have had to enter into a marriage without love, you are now free to do as you wish with your life. Woollerson is yours whether you marry or not. I only wish for two things, Kathryn—your happiness and the preservation of Woollerson. God bless you. Gran.'

When Mr Barnes had gone, Kathryn stayed exactly where she was, sitting motionless, her face drained of colour, the letter clutched in one hand, as wild thoughts raced in a stupefying jumble through her suddenly aching head. Many different emotions swept over her outwardly calm exterior, but it was some time before she had the honesty to admit to herself that, strangely, relief was not one of them. 'Why, why aren't I glad, even at this eleventh hour, that Gran has given me a way out?' she asked herself. 'I should be shouting for joy, shouldn't I? I must tell Zac at once, of course. I wonder where he is.' Slowly she folded the letter and put it back in its envelope, then slipped it into the pocket of her skirt and stood up, acutely aware of the indisputable fact that the letter had increased her sense of panic and confusion a thousandfold, rather than bring her comfort and release from a distasteful arrangement which had been forced upon her against her will. 'Oh, Gran,' she said aloud, 'what a lot of trouble you've caused. What a mess it all is!' She had to force herself to walk towards the door and then to open it, almost as if she knew full well that Zac would be standing not twenty feet from her, staring across at her from the doorway of the office.

'What's up, Kathryn?' he asked when he saw her. 'You're as white as a ghost!' He came swiftly across the hall and took both her hands in his. 'What did old Barnes want? I saw him leave.'

'You'd better come in here a minute,' she said, having to clear her throat before any words would form themselves. 'I've got to talk to you.' To her anguished surprise he let go of her hands and put a comforting arm round her shoulders as she turned and went back into the drawing-room. She longed to rest her head against him and had to make a conscious effort to hold herself aloof.

'Sit down before you fall down,' Zac advised, leading her to the sofa and pushing her gently down. Then he went and leant against the mantelpiece and looked down at her bent head. 'Now tell me what's the matter.'

In an agony of indecision, Kathryn looked up at him. She could feel the letter in her pocket and it crackled slightly when she moved. She opened her mouth to say the fateful words, indeed her hand went to her pocket in the act of taking the letter out and showing it to him, but the words she uttered when they came were not what she had intended them to be, and even as she heard herself speak she wondered how she could be so deceitful. 'It's nothing really. Nothing to do with Mr Barnes, at any rate. He just wanted to know what time he should be here on ... on the day. I think I've probably just got a bad case of wedding nerves.' And what about the letter, an inner voice cried, aren't you going to tell him about the letter? 'I know I'm being stupid,' she went on quickly, 'but I think I've only just realised that there are only two weeks to go.'

'Is that really all?' Zac questioned, his eyes narrowing. 'Old Barnes didn't have some nasty little surprise he'd been saving up to spring on you at the last minute?'

'No.' She could hardly believe her own ears when she heard herself repeat the lie and her voice was almost inaudible. 'No, nothing like that.'

'Well then, cheer up.' He moved to the sofa and, sitting down beside her, took one of her hands in his. 'Don't crack up at the eleventh hour. Unless ...' He paused and she felt his grip on her hand tighten. 'Unless you want to back out. You still can, you know.' His words twisted the knife further and she stared at him dumbly. 'But if that's really what this is all about, tell me now while there's still time. *Is* that what you want?'

Silently she continued to stare at him, her grey eyes looking steadily into his. Then she slowly shook her head. 'No, that's not what I want, Zac.' Their gazes held and she felt him move beside her, and suddenly she knew what he was going to do, and she knew too that she had been waiting and longing for this to happen ever since the night of Mr Eliot's party—and as Zac took her in his arms and his mouth came down to find hers, she admitted once and for all that there was no longer any doubt in her mind about her reason for failing so dishonestly to tell him about the letter.

CHAPTER SIX

IT was generally agreed afterwards that it was a lovely wedding. The bride looked stunning, the bridesmaids attractive, but not to such an extent as to detract from the impact made by the bride, and the bridegroom was charm itself and inordinately handsome in his formal attire. The sun shone as brightly as any bride could have hoped and everyone enjoyed themselves, including herself, as Kathryn acknowledged privately, having decided beforehand that she would regard the proceedings—or at least the reception—as a lovely party and a celebration of the fact that Woollerson had been saved. Almost incredibly she had somehow managed to put all thoughts of the letter so far to the back of her mind that she had virtually succeeded in convincing herself that it had never existed and that she had indeed been forced to marry to save the estate. The service in the pretty little village church had gone without a hitch and she had made her responses in a clear voice, knowing that for her part her promises were sincere and that she had every intention of keeping them. She was absolutely determined that their marriage would be a success, and she hoped that in time Zac might grow to love her as she had already begun to love him.

His friends from Ireland had all come over together on the boat, landing at Holyhead on the previous evening and driving across to Suffolk in the morning. They were a noisy and very friendly crowd and went out of their way to be nice to her, issuing invitations for her and Zac to visit them at some vague unspecified time in the future and generally livening up the proceedings a good deal. They drank a lot and laughed a lot, and when, to her complete and utter surprise, Zac whisked her away for a totally unexpected honeymoon, she was sure that it was his friends who were responsible for the long string of old tin cans, paper streamers and old shoes that trailed behind the car as they drove away down the drive.

'What on earth are we doing?' she asked, turning to Zac from where he had dumped her in the car beside him. She was half laughing because of the antics of his crazy friends, who were running along beside the car and in imminent danger of being run down, shouting ribald remarks and highly suggestive jokes as the car gathered speed. 'Zac, I'm still in my wedding dress!'

'And very beautiful you look too, my love,' he said, very sensibly keeping his eyes on the road. 'We're going on our honeymoon, of course. What else?'

'I rather guessed that.' She sat back and grinned across at him. 'But it's usual to change first, you know. And why didn't I know anything about it?'

'You were so obviously not expecting anything that I thought it would be nice to surprise you.' He still didn't look at her, so she was free to study his face, and she knew that the more she looked at it the more she liked what she saw.

'It was nice, and you've certainly surprised

me. Good heavens, where are we going now?' She saw that they had turned off the main road and were currently bumping along the track leading to the cottage where Mr and Mrs Roberts now lived.

Zac's only answer was to smile across at her and then return his attention to guiding the car over the ruts until they pulled up outside the cottage. Kathryn saw without paying particular attention that what looked like a brand new MGB was already parked outside the cottage, and she wondered who was visiting the Roberts's, but then she turned her attention to Zac. who had got out of the car and was holding the passenger door open for her. 'Come on,' he said, 'out you get.'

Frowning in puzzlement, Kathryn gathered up the skirts of her beautiful creamy lace dress and followed Zac into the cottage. 'We're changing here,' he said by way of explanation. 'Your clothes are upstairs.'

'Curiouser and curiouser,' she remarked as she climbed the narrow stairs, but there was a smile on her face and she felt suddenly extraordinarily happy. Mr and Mrs Roberts, she knew, would still be at the reception, but she was both touched and amazed that Zac should have gone to the trouble of planning all this with the obvious connivance of the old couple and probably other people as well. In the small back bedroom she found her clothes laid out for her on the bed, the same flannel suit and blouse that she had worn when they had gone to London to buy her ring and most suitable for the time of year. 'Who decided what I should wear?' she called down the stairs, half laughing and already reaching behind her for the zip at the back of her dress.

'Mary. She packed a case for you too. How are you doing?' Zac appeared at the bottom of the stairs and she saw that his morning suit had already been discarded in favour of well-cut slacks and a striped shirt which he was in the act of buttoning up.

'The zip seems to have stuck,' she answered. 'Would you mind?' And in a moment he was standing behind her, gently easing the recalcitrant zip upwards, until the small piece of lace which had been caught was freed, and then sliding it carefully all the way down her back. 'Thank you.'

She quickly put her hands up and caught the dress before it fell to the floor, thinking that she must surely have imagined that his hands had trembled slightly when they inadvertently touched her bare flesh. Certainly they were quite steady as they came to rest on her shoulders, then gently turned her round to face him. Although she held the dress in front of her, the upper half of her firm young breasts and the deep cleft between them were clearly visible, and she saw his eyes rest briefly on them before he raised them again and looked steadily at her. 'Happy, Mrs Wilding?'

Kathryn had a split second in which to decide how to answer. Instinct told her to fling her arms round his neck and tell him there and then of her true feelings, but prudence demanded that she continue to keep their relationship on a basis no higher than friendship, and she therefore chose to return a casual answer to his apparently serious question. 'Of course I am,' she said lightly, moving away from him. 'It was a fabulous wedding, wasn't it? And I liked your friends, particularly John Reilly and his wife. Did you know they'd asked us to visit them in Ireland?'

There was a perceptible pause as he turned on his heel and started down the stairs. 'No, I didn't,' he said rather curtly. 'It's quite out of the question, of course.'

Kathryn carefully laid her dress on the bed and hurried into her blouse and skirt before going back to the top of the stairs and calling down. 'Why? Why is it out of the question? I thought it would be rather fun.'

He answered her from the sitting-room but without coming to the open door to speak. 'We couldn't spare the time. I've got my hands full licking the estate into shape.'

His tone did not invite further comment and she wished she hadn't mentioned the invitation. She told herself that she ought to have had more tact, knowing perfectly well that Ireland was an emotive topic of conversation with him. 'Perhaps we could go later,' she said, more to fill an awkward little silence than because she felt that it was very likely that they would ever go.

'Perhaps.' Suddenly he appeared in the doorway and frowned up at her. 'Aren't you ready yet?'

'Yes, I am.' Quickly she shrugged into the jacket of her suit, picked up her bag and after a last lingering look at her lovely dress, hurried down the stairs and joined him in the sitting-room. 'Sorry to have kept you waiting.'

To her relief Zac smiled. 'You're always worth waiting for, my love.' She saw that he was jingling the car keys in his hand as he eyed her up and down. 'Here, catch!' He threw the keys at her and she automatically put out her hand and caught them.

She looked at him in surprise. 'Do you want me to drive?' He'd always made it clear that when they went anywhere together he was the one who would be doing the driving.

He shook his head as he continued to grin at her. 'Not particularly.'

'Then why give me the keys?' Really, he was suddenly behaving very oddly.

'Because, my dear wife, those are not the keys to the car in which we arrived here. They belong to your new car, which is waiting for you outside. Come on.' Her jaw dropped as she followed him out into the open. He walked over to the gleaming white sports car which she had noticed upon their arrival and which she had naturally assumed belonged to someone visiting the Roberts's. 'My wedding present to you, Kathryn,' he said, turning and smiling at the dumbfounded expression on her face. 'I hope you like it.'

Almost as if she was sleepwalking, too amazed to believe his words, she slowly approached the car, then put out her hand to touch the shining paintwork. Then she looked up at him, a deep frown creasing her forehead. 'Are you serious, Zac?' she asked. 'Is it really for me? I can't believe it! It must have cost a fortune!'

'Never mind about that,' he said impatiently. 'Do you like it?'

'*Like* it? Of course I do! I'd have to be completely round the bend if I didn't. But you make me feel terrible. I haven't got anything for you—I'm afraid it never occurred to me. Oh, Zac, it's really far too generous!' But in spite of her discomfiture she was quite unable to hide her sheer delight at the total unexpectedness of his extravagant present, and this time she let her heart rule her head as she turned to him and, standing on her toes, quickly kissed him on the cheek. 'Thank you so very much.' She had intended to move away from him at once, but his arms went round her and she felt her feet leave the ground as he lifted her against him, suspended effortlessly in space, as his mouth sought hers in a long possessive kiss. Immediately her pulse began to race and her blood surged hotly through her veins. If her arms had not been imprisoned against his chest they would have wrapped themselves round his neck and her hands would have been in his thick black hair, but crushed as she was against his male hardness all she could do was return his kiss and try to show him by the movement of her mouth alone that she was ready and more than willing to meet him halfway.

But he soon withdrew his lips from hers and set her feet firmly on the ground once more. His breathing was a fraction faster than normal, but in no other way did he give her any reason to believe that she was expected to read anything of any particular significance into his recent actions. Indeed, his words soon told her exactly where she stood. 'That'll do,' he said. 'I accept your thanks.' His tone was almost that of a slightly exasperated father admonishing an over-exuberant child, and Kathryn closed her eyes for a moment to give herself time to recover, sickeningly aware of how near she had come to betraying her feelings.

She took a deep breath and turned and opened the car door. 'If it's really mine,' she said in a surprisingly normal voice, 'I hope you're going to let me drive it. I presume we're going away in it?'

'Yes, I thought we would. And yes, I suppose I'll have to let you drive.' His sigh of resignation was exaggerated and had the blessed effect of putting their relationship back on to its usual plane once more. 'I'll just shut the front door, then we'll be on our way. The suitcases are in the boot, by the way.'

While he went to make sure that they'd left nothing behind in the cottage and to see that the door was shut, Kathryn spent the time familiarising herself with the positions of the various knobs and levers, trying out the windscreen washers and the indicators and frankly revelling in the newness of everything. The unmistakable smell of the virgin black rubber of the floor covering, the dull sheen of the black upholstery and the gleaming chrome excited her, and she was suddenly impatient to be off, driving for the first time in her own brand new car which had been so generously given to her by her own brand new husband. As Zac took his seat beside her, she switched on and smiled in appreciation when the engine sprang immediately into life and she was able to move off at once, expertly executing the necessary turn in front of the cottage, then changing into a higher gear as they quickly left the cottage behind.

'Happy?'

She had felt Zac's eyes on her and wondered what he was thinking. 'You've asked me that once already,' she replied, keeping her eyes on the track, 'and the answer's still the same. Of course I am. This is the most fantastic present I've ever had in my whole life, and I shall never be able to thank you enough.' Her answer assumed that his question had been connected with the car and nothing of deeper significance. They reached the end of the track and she looked across at him. 'Which way? Where are we going?'

He sat back in his seat and crossed his legs before answering with a grin. 'I haven't the faintest idea.'

'What?' Her eyes widened in surprise.

'I had no idea where you might like to go, so I didn't book anywhere. As it's September I'm sure we won't have any problems. I thought we'd just drive and when we feel like stopping we'll stop. So just keep going in any direction you choose and in about an hour's time we'll start looking for a decent hotel. We'll be getting hungry by then anyway. I don't suppose you ate much during the reception, did you? I know I didn't.'

'Now you mention it, no, I didn't.' Deciding at random, Kathryn turned right on to the main road and quickly moved the car into top gear. She found the car very smooth and easy to drive, which was just as well, because Zac's mention of a hotel had started her off on a whole new train of thought and she needed time to think ahead and to try and work out how she was going to handle the inevitable moment which was looming ever nearer, without having to concentrate one hundred per cent on the mechanics of driving a car which was unfamiliar to her.

But it was as if he had read her mind; perhaps her expression had given her thoughts away. 'To set your mind at rest, Mrs Wilding,' he said from the seat beside her, a mocking note in his voice, 'we will of course ask for separate rooms and if, heaven forbid, there are none available, then we'll insist on twin beds. Will that satisfy you?'

'Yes, I suppose it'll have to.' Her answer was a trifle breathless.

'You don't really expect me to go to the expense of two separate double rooms, do you?' he asked, his voice suddenly impatient.

'No. No, I suppose not,' she agreed after an awkward pause. 'But ... er ... oh, dear ...' She felt her cheeks begin to burn and didn't know how to go on.

'What is it now?' he asked wearily. 'What's going on in that strange head of yours? Better tell me now, rather than in front of some hotel manager.'

In acute embarrassment, she gripped the steering wheel and found that her hands were sweating as they slipped on the shiny new surface. 'Well, it just seems so strange to think of sharing a bedroom with you, that's all.' The words came out jerkily and she felt incredibly foolish. 'Suddenly I don't feel I know you well enough.' Her reaction to his shout of laughter was half irritation and half relief. 'I mean ... well, it's a bit intimate, isn't it?'

'Good lord, is that all? You funny little innocent!' Zac leant back in his seat and gave way to another burst of laughter.

'Stop it, you beast! I'm serious—and embarrassed.' Kathryn wished he'd stop laughing at her, because she was feeling more idiotic by the minute, and for the life of her, she couldn't see anything particulary funny in what she had said.

'O.K. I'm sorry.' He cleared his throat and sat up. 'But, to use the word you used, marriage is inclined to be a bit intimate at times, you know, or so they tell me. But don't worry, I have no intention of embarrassing you. We'll work something out. Now get a move on, girl, unless you want to spend your honeymoon in Haversham!'

In the event, it was hunger that forced them to stop. They were well into Norfolk and driving along the coast road when Zac suggested that they stop at the first decent looking pub they came to. 'We'll have something to eat and then decide whether we push on and find something better for the night,' he said as she obediently pulled into the small car park belonging to a long, low and very old inn, pink-washed and very pretty in the light of the setting sun. A hanging sign informed them that food was available, and mouthwatering smells assailed their nostrils as they made their way through the bar and into the dining-room, where soon they were tucking into large and generous platefuls of home-made steak, kidney and mushroom pie, tender runner beans grown on the premises by the landlord and beautifully cooked crunchy roast potatoes. This was followed by a rich and creamy trifle and with the meal they shared a bottle of surprisingly good Beaujolais.

Only when their plates had been cleared away and they were sitting drinking their coffee did either of them utter more than a few words. 'I honestly can't remember when I tasted anything quite so good,' Kathryn said with a contented sigh. 'In fact,' she added, looking across at Zac a little hazily, 'I think that was the best meal I've ever had in my life!'

He grinned back at her. 'It would appear that you also enjoyed the wine.'

She gave a small giggle and leant towards him confidentially. 'I don't think I've got a very good head for drink,' she said, enunciating her words with care. 'I feel lovely, all warm and woozy. It's a very nice feeling.'

He regarded her with mock solemnity for a few moments. 'I think that's made the decision for us, then,' he said, standing up. 'No, don't move. I'm going to see if they can put us up for the night.'

Kathryn stayed where she was, drinking her coffee, hot, strong and black, yet feeling more drowsy by the minute. She hoped they'd have a room for them, feeling very disinclined to go any further, and her earlier misgivings about sharing a room with her husband of a few hours seemed to have disappeared. Zac soon returned, saying that it was all fixed and that they could stay and he sat down and poured himself another cup of coffee, while she sat looking at him enquiringly. 'Well, aren't you going to tell me?' she asked at last, when it became apparent that he wasn't going to add anything to his statement.

'Tell you what?' He looked at her with an innocent look on his face which was belied by the glint of amusement in his eyes.

'How many beds, of course.' In her slightly fuddled state she spoke louder than she had intended, and the only other people in the dining-room, a young couple on the far side of the room, looked up and the man laughed.

'Be quiet, woman,' he said mildly. 'You've

definitely had too much to drink. And the answer to your question is one, I'm afraid.'

'Oh, you poor darling,' she said, not bothering to lower her voice at all. 'You'll have to sleep on the floor, then, won't you?'

'Shut up, Kathryn, and have some more of that coffee, for God's sake!'

'I'd rather have some more wine. I'm enjoying myself.'

'And so am I, but I'm not sure if I will be for much longer. And as for your having any more wine—not a chance!' Then he frowned. 'I wonder why it's gone to your head to such an extent? Did you have any lunch?'

Kathryn wrinkled her brow in an effort to remember. 'Sort of—I think. No, I remember, I couldn't really eat anything. There were too many butterflies in my stomach at the time. What about you?'

'Mine was mainly liquid, I'm afraid, with John and Sue Reilly at the Red Lion.'

'Oh, yes, the good old Red Lion. Your harem will miss you tonight.' He didn't reply and there was silence for a few minutes as they sipped their coffee. 'I expect you broke a few hearts today,' she said at length, 'by marrying me, I mean.' She could still feel the wine, but her head was gradually becoming clearer and just at that moment it struck her forcibly that a lot of people might consider Zac's action in marrying her without being in love to be immoral. 'You could say it was a crime, really.'

Zac pointedly looked at his watch. 'I think it's time you went to bed,' he said. 'You're talking absolute nonsense.'

'But I don't want to go to bed,' she protested. 'It's much too early.'

'All right, then,' he sighed. 'If you think you can make it, let's go for a walk. The air might clear your head.'

He took her arm in a firm grip as they left the inn and she was soon glad of it, because quite apart from being just a little bit unsteady on her feet, they had walked no more than a hundred yards before they were plunged into complete and impenetrable darkness. The inn was off the main road and there were no street lights to guide them, so they stopped by common consent in order to give their eyes time to get used to the dark, then walked on slowly in the coolness of the night air. 'This is nice,' Kathryn said almost in a whisper, feeling that to speak in a normal voice would be something like sacrilege in the total silence which enveloped them. 'A bit spooky, but nice.'

Zac only grunted in reply, but he slipped his arm round her waist and held her close to his side as her long legs kept pace with his leisurely stride. Then he stopped and drew her to a halt. 'Look up, Kathryn, above your head,' he said quietly. 'Quite a sight, isn't it?'

She did as he said and drank in the magical sight of a million stars shining down at them from the midnight-blue backcloth of the night sky. 'It's beautiful,' she murmured. 'Quite incredible!' As she lowered her gaze once more to seek out the pale blur of his face in the surrounding darkness, she felt herself being pulled forcefully into his arms, and her lips gladly parted under the sudden onslaught of his almost brutally demanding mouth on hers. Her head swam as she leant against him, and his kiss seemed to go on for ever. Then she felt him push her over towards the side of the road where there was a low wall and he took his mouth away from hers for a moment as he put one foot on the wall, then bent her back over his thigh, steadying her with one arm behind her shoulders, and his mouth came down hard on hers again while his free hand roughly pulled her blouse from the restraining waistband of her skirt, quickly pushing upwards until it found the silken barrier of her bra, which in turn was swiftly pushed out of the way until his hand closed convulsively round the satin smoothness of her breast.

She felt him shudder against her and she moaned as his passion communicated itself to her until she felt that she didn't care what he did to her, there and then if that was what he wanted, so long as he went on caressing her bare flesh so intimately and his mouth probed ever deeper into the delights beyond the open archway of her pliant lips. Her hands reached out to him, first burying themselves in the thick blackness of his hair and then dropping down the length of his back as she felt the heat of his body through the thin material of his shirt. Then she too found a way in so that her hands were touching the heady smoothness of the firm taut flesh which sheathed his back and shoulders, then creeping round to play with the forest of dark hair that covered his broad chest.

Then all at once his hands were still and his lips abruptly softened against hers, and she pressed herself with increasing urgency against him, begging him with her body to go on, but he took his hand from her breast and steadied her with his other arm as he returned his foot to the ground and straightened up. 'Let's go back,' he said quietly, and her moment of disappointment and frustration immediately gave way to a renewed flare of excitement at the promise she read into his words. She swayed slightly towards him on legs which were still not quite steady and gladly grasped the hand he held out to her as they walked back together.

When they were in the warm and friendly atmosphere of the inn once more, she needed no urging towards the stairs. 'You go to bed,' Zac said quietly. 'I'll be up soon.' And he watched her start up the stairs before turning and going through to the bar. As she climbed the stairs, Kathryn wished with all her heart that she had not drunk quite so much wine at dinner. Her head was aching dully and her legs still felt as if they were stuffed with cotton wool, but underlying everything was the intoxicating sensation of newly aroused passion, enveloping her in a primed awareness of a fulfilment at present beyond her experience, only needing the vital spark from Zac to bring her to an explosion of passion and ecstasy which, in her innocence and ignorance, she nevertheless felt must surely rock her to her very foundations.

Once upstairs she found their room and, quickly taking out of her case only what she would need for the night, undressed and slipped into her dressing-gown, then went in search of the bathroom. A quick bath would refresh her, she thought, and perhaps make her more alert. She was aware of a sleepy languor creeping over her and she very much wanted to fight it and bring herself fully awake. Zac had left her with the definite impression that there was more than a possibility that their wedding night would after all be a traditional one and not the empty mockery she had sadly but resignedly expected it to be. All her maidenly modesty and inhibitions had been ruthlessly swept aside by the raw passion she had seen unleashed in the darkness such a short time ago, and although she mentally shied away from examining too closely his motives for wanting her, she felt instinctively that it would cement the new bond between them more surely and more permanently than anything else if she were to lose her virginity that night.

She shivered suddenly, although the bath water was still hot, and she quickly pulled out the plug and stood up as the water level rapidly dropped, reaching for the large bath towel which the hotel had provided. She had left her wristwatch in their room, but she judged that she could not have been more than a quarter of an hour, but all the same she hurriedly dried herself and slipped into her nightdress and dressing-gown and left the bathroom. She wanted to be safely in bed when Zac came up, and as she approached the door to their room she hoped she hadn't taken too long over her bath. But to her relief the room was empty, and she quickly ran a comb through her slightly damp hair, took off her dressing-gown and got into bed, thinking as she did so that it was a stroke of luck that the small inn had only been able to offer them a room with a double bed. Then she smiled as she remembered her earlier misgivings and her absurd suggestion that Zac would have to sleep on the floor, and she knew that it was his sexual urgency out there in the darkness under the magical almost unearthly beauty of the night sky which had drawn from her a longing, yearning response, which in turn had turned her attitudes upside down.

She yawned widely and snuggled further down under the covers. It was a comfortable bed and the sheets were smooth and velvety where they touched her bare flesh. She wished Zac would come and wondered why he was taking so long. Surely he must know that she would be in bed by now? She yawned again as she turned her head on the pillow to look at her watch, then with a small frown she settled on her side, facing towards the door so that she would see him as soon as he came into the room. Her eyelids began to droop and she forced her eyes open wide and fixed them on the door which obstinately remained firmly closed, but, try as she would, she was quite unable to prevent them from gradually closing again, and her last thought as she unknowingly drifted over the invisible border which lay between waking and sleeping was that it was absolutely vital that she stay awake.

CHAPTER SEVEN

SHE awoke next morning with an immediate but initially unspecified feeling of unease, but in the first moments of awareness she was completely disorientated and wondered where on earth she

was. She rolled over on to her back and stretched
her arms out on either side of her in the big bed,
and it was then that her feeling that all was not
well crystallised into a sharp pang of anguish as
she swiftly turned her head and saw that the other
half of the bed was unoccupied. With a groan she
sat up and looked desperately round the room, as
if by doing so she could conjure Zac up out of
nowhere and tell him at once how sorry she was
that she had fallen asleep at such an important
moment in their new life together. A dull misery
swept over her as she looked again at his side of
the bed, wondering whether he had actually slept
with her at all, but it was immediately obvious that
he had. She could distinctly make out the
indentation made by his head on the pillow, and
with a cry of desolation she flung herself down,
burying her head in his pillow and breathing in the
unique masculine smell of him as a feeling of
foreboding overcame her. She was suddenly
convinced that by falling asleep she had robbed
both him and herself of their one, infinitely
precious, chance of happiness.

Locked in bitter mortification, she didn't hear
the door open, and her heart seemed to stop
beating for a long moment when she heard his
voice. 'Are you awake, Kathryn?' His words
lacked any expression and she forced herself to
stretch and pretend to yawn as she turned over
and looked at him. She saw that he was standing a
few yards from the bed, fully dressed and
regarding her with expressionless eyes, and she
said the first words that came into her head. 'Have
you been up long? What time is it?'

'I've been up since about six o'clock, and it's

now a quarter past eight,' he answered, looking away from her and walking over to the window to draw back the curtains. 'Did you sleep well?'

Feeling the hot colour flooding her face, Kathryn swallowed before answering. 'Yes, very well, thank you—too well, I'm afraid. Zac, I'm sorry . . .'

She was startled by the bite in the words as he cut her short. 'There's nothing to be sorry about. You were tired and had had far too much to drink. I suggest we don't refer to it again.' He turned abruptly on his heel and walked towards the door. 'I'll see you downstairs. We can have breakfast any time we like.'

He already had the door open and was halfway through it before she spoke again. 'Please don't go like that, Zac,' she implored him. 'I want to talk to you!' Her eyes pleaded with him to stay and she watched in deep distress as he began to close the door.

'But I don't want to talk to you, my dear,' he said very quietly. 'Not about last night, at any rate.' The door closed firmly behind him and she was left sitting huddled wretchedly in the bed, staring fixedly at the door, knowing that she had been horribly and painfully right in thinking they had missed their chance of happiness. In her moment of need her stern upbringing came to her aid and she did not give way to the avalanche of bitter tears that was hovering close to the edge of her self-control, and instead she carefully and slowly pushed back the bedclothes and got out of bed. The only way to get through the next few hours, she thought, would be to pretend that nothing untoward had happend the previous night. All thought of his passion, of his hard masculine body pressed against hers, of the promise of his kisses, must be pushed right out of her mind as if it had been two quite different people who had been locked together in the darkness, on the brink of becoming lovers in the magic of the night. Nothing could bring those moments of ecstasy back and they were best forgotten.

Pulling herself together with an impatient shake, she crossed to where her suitcase lay open on the floor and bent to examine its contents, wondering just what Mary had packed for her. She was pleased with what she found and quickly extracted a white linen trouser suit and a black silk blouse. Apart from wanting to look her best, she also wanted Zac to be proud of his wife, and when she went downstairs twenty minutes later no one would have guessed at the misery behind her smiling eyes or the hard knot of anguish and regret that was gripping her stomach muscles and making her feel sick. Zac had his head buried in the morning paper and did not see her until she was standing right beside him.

'I hope I haven't been too long,' she said brightly, only briefly meeting his eyes. 'Shall we go in to breakfast?'

Without a word he put down his paper and followed her into the dining-room, but Kathryn felt that the effort she had made had been worthwhile when she saw a faint smile on his face as he took his seat opposite her and broke the silence between them. 'You look good,' he told her. 'I like the outfit.'

'Thank you.' She was relieved to hear the

approach of the landlord's wife who was coming to take their order. 'Just grapefruit, coffee and toast for me, please,' she said, knowing that a cooked breakfast would have been quite beyond her at that moment, but oddly pleased to note that Zac's appetite was unimpaired.

'Have you thought about where you want to go?' he asked some time later, having demolished a large plate of bacon and eggs and sounding his usual self.

'No, I haven't. I don't mind,' she answered. Anywhere so long as I'm with you, she added to herself. Perhaps I'll get another chance, and if I do I swear I won't make a mess of things a second time. 'Let's just keep driving, shall we? At least the weather's good.' Fancy being reduced to talking about the weather on your honeymoon, she thought ruefully.

Half an hour later, seated beside Zac who was driving, and with the pretty little inn far behind them, she felt her spirits begin to rise. The sun shone brightly overhead and there was very little traffic on the roads. They had decided to keep away from motorways and main roads and the minor roads and leafy lanes led them through pretty villages and small towns which they would otherwise have missed. They stopped for lunch at a hotel in Blakeney and after their meal strolled through the small village, mingling with the fishermen, the sailing fraternity and the dedicated birdwatchers who had come to catch a glimpse of the wildlife for which the place was rightly famous. Suddenly Kathryn caught sight of herself in a shop window and, muttering something to Zac about feeling overdressed, dived into the shop, emerging some time later clad in jeans and a tee-shirt and carrying the white trouser suit and silk blouse in a carrier bag.

Zac grinned when he saw her. 'You look about sixteen in that get-up,' he said. 'What was all that about?'

'I suddenly felt out of place,' she answered, falling into step beside him as they continued their stroll down to where the boats were moored. 'Now I feel as if I'm really on holiday.' Impulsively she took his hand. 'Zac, let's enjoy ourselves,' she urged, halting their progress and staring up into his face. 'We're right away from Woollerson and anyone we know. Let's really try and have a good time.'

Not liking to admit to herself how much his answer would mean to her, she waited as he looked quizzically down at her upturned face. Then he raised his free hand and carefully tucked an errant strand of golden hair behind her ear, smiling slowly as he did so. 'Of course we will,' he said, and his voice was kind. 'Don't worry so, Kathryn. Things will work themselves out.'

She let go of his hand then and dropped her eyes as she felt the undoubted meaning behind his words bring the telltale colour to her cheeks. 'I like the feel of this place,' she said quickly to cover her confusion, walking on down the narrow main street towards the quayside. 'In fact I wouldn't mind staying here for a day or two. What do you think?' They had reached the harbour and stood looking down at the collection of yachts and small boats temporarily marooned on the mud-flats which had been exposed by the receding tide.

'Certainly, if that's what you want,' he replied.

'You're right, there is something about the place that gets to you. Come on, let's go for a walk.'

They walked along a narrow grass-covered bank which ran through the mud-flats and into the marshes until they were away from the sounds of the little port. The cries of seabirds were all around them and the only people they saw were serious-faced birdwatchers, dressed in serviceable tweeds and stout walking shoes, powerful-looking binoculars slung round their necks and with few words exchanged for fear of disturbing the wildlife. Here and there the delicate mauve of sea-lavender added a touch of colour to the brown and green of the salt marshes, the tightly packed flowers in flat-topped clusters waving gently in the breeze. The air was strong and tangy with salt and Kathryn breathed in deeply, a feeling of ease and contentment stealing over her as she followed Zac through the long coarse grass. They spoke very little and when they did their voices were muted, out of tacit respect for the rare birds and those who wished to observe them.

When they were tired they stopped and lay down on the grass, the warmth of the sun soon inducing in them both a taste of semi-somnolence and a delicious languor. They were in no hurry to do anything, time stretching before them un-hampered by the usual restrictions brought about by the necessity to work and attend to their normal duties, and they lay side by side contentedly listening to the birds and the gentle sighing of the light wind in the grass above their heads. After a while Kathryn became aware that Zac's breathing had deepened and taken on the evenness of sleep, and she carefully propped herself on one elbow and gazed down at the face of the man whom only the day before she had promised to love, honour and keep in sickness and in health. Her heart skipped a beat as she thought back to the wedding service, remembering how she had felt as she stood beside him in the packed little church and made her vows, knowing that in that moment she had given herself to him wholeheartedly and sincerely, although he was completely unaware of the fact and for his part had only been sticking to his part of their bargain.

Her eyes dropped to the wide gold band on the third finger of her left hand, and as she twisted it round and round on her finger the sun caught it and threw shafts of brilliance into her eyes, dazzling her and forcing her to look away and back at Zac. She realised that she had never seen him off guard before and she was startled by the change in him. The deep lines that normally marked his face were smoothed out and his mouth which was so often clamped into a hard and uncompromising firmness was relaxed, almost gentle. His dark hair was ruffled above his deeply-tanned face and she longed to reach out and smooth it into place. Her eyes travelled down the length of the tall and virile man lying beside her, then returned to his face and in particular to his mouth, and she bent silently, swiftly brushing his lips with hers, then gasped in fright as she felt his arms go round her and hug her so hard against him that all the breath was knocked out of her body.

In one swift movement and with her slender body still crushed against him, Zac rolled over until she was lying beneath him, then his mouth came down on hers cruelly and savagely and she sensed the sudden anger in him. As abruptly as he had seized her he let her go and sat up. 'That will teach you, dear wife,' he said, and she was dismayed at the bitterness in his voice, 'not to handle the goods if you don't want them.'

'But I . . .' she began to protest, but he cut her short, standing up and pulling her roughly to her feet.

'Come on,' he said curtly, 'If you want to stay here we'd better see about booking a room.'

'Zac! Don't be like this, please!' But she was speaking to his rapidly retreating back, and she ran to catch him up.

'Shut up!' he snapped over his shoulder. 'It's time you learnt when to keep quiet!'

'How dare you speak to me like that!' Suddenly she was furiously angry and glared at the broad back marching purposefully away from her. 'Who the hell do you think you are!'

At that, he suddenly stopped and turned round so that she almost ran into him, and he seized both her wrists in one large hand, holding her in front of him while he looked down at her. 'Ah, I see the old Kathryn has reappeared,' he said softly. 'It didn't take long, did it?' Childishly she kicked out in the direction of his shins, but her foot did not make contact as he merely moved out of range, holding her at arm's length. 'I'll tell you just who the hell I am, Kathryn my dear,' he went on calmly. 'Your husband, and a very Victorian one at that. You know the old saying about a woman, a dog and a walnut tree, don't you?' He waited for her to answer, but none was forthcoming. 'No? Well then, allow me to enlighten you. The more you beat 'em the better they be. As a matter of fact I think I'll give you a small sample right now.' And almost before she could guess what was in his mind, he dropped the carrier bag which contained her white trouser suit and which he had been carrying for her on to the ground, thus freeing his other hand in order to give her a hearty slap on her bottom. Then he let her go and, bending unconcernedly to pick up the carrier bag once more, turned and walked on.

'You bastard!' Kathryn stood where she was, furiously rubbing her sore behind and watching him walk away from her. She opened her mouth to hurl further abuse after him, but a serious-faced couple of birdwatchers suddenly appeared out of nowhere and gave her a reproachful look for making so much noise, so she closed her mouth again and hurried after Zac in furious silence. But she deliberately kept her distance and did not allow herself to catch up with him until he had reached the hotel where they had lunched, when she followed him inside and stood silently by his side as he booked a double room with bath, the receptionist having informed him that they had no single rooms at all since they found there was virtually no demand for them.

When the porter had opened the door to their room and Zac stood aside for her to precede him, Kathryn's feelings were an equal mixture of relief and disappointment when she walked into the large and prettily-furnished room overlooking the harbour and saw the twin beds, and she was careful to avoid looking at Zac. She was still smarting both literally and metaphorically from his chastisement and certainly didn't want to get involved in any discussion about sleeping arrangements. Too late, she realised that they should have foreseen this particular pitfall before they set out and come to some arrangement which would have avoided any embarrassment. She felt most acutely the ambivalence of her position, being a wife and yet not a wife, and the world in general was bound to jump to wrong conclusions and make erroneous assumptions. As for Zac, she thought with a sudden renewed spurt of irritation, she was convinced that he found it all highly amusing, and the more she showed her embarrassment the more hilarious he appeared to find it.

The next few days passed in an uneasy truce. To give him his due, Zac was the soul of tact when it came to intimate occasions such as undressing and bathing, invariably making it easy for her by disappearing at the appropriate times, and she was, she supposed, grudgingly grateful to him for it. He had made no further advances to her whatever and they were for the most part polite and rather distant with each other. Their days were spent exploring the village, going for long walks and sometimes driving out into the surrounding countryside for lunch or tea, but never going very far. The weather held and gradually she relaxed, getting used to Zac's continual presence and to the fact that their strange half-marriage was an established fact. It no longer appeared that Zac had any intention of deepening the relationship, and Kathryn was learning to live with the aching regret she felt at the thought of what might have been had she not fallen asleep on their wedding night. Although she was now convinced that Zac's lovemaking in the darkness of that night had been prompted by nothing more than a masculine desire for sex, she wished with all her heart that she had not thrown away the chance of showing him her true feelings and perhaps even drawing from him something more than he had intended to give.

On their exploration of Blakeney itself they had come across a row of old flint-built cottages, carefully restored and available for holiday lettings, fully furnished and equipped, and Kathryn had been tempted to suggest that they take one for the remainder of their holiday, thinking that a greater privacy might bring them closer, but at the last minute her courage failed her and she said nothing. And so the days slipped by until suddenly there were no more left and they were in the car once more, heading for home.

'Well, Mrs Wilding,' Zac's voice jolted her out of her thoughts, 'glad to be going home?'

'Yes,' she lied. 'It will be good to see old Bess again.' That at least was true. Something was niggling at the back of her mind, but she couldn't put her finger on just what it was. She felt sure that it was important and that she should have thought of it before, but it wasn't until they drew up outside Woollerson Hall and they were being greeted by the staff who were standing in the doorway to welcome them home that she realised what it was.

'We've prepared the master suite for you, Miss Kathryn,' Mary told her as they went inside. 'We thought that would be what you'd want now that you're married. I hope we did right?'

Kathryn turned a gasp into a cough as she felt her colour rise. 'Yes, of course,' she murmured, not daring to look behind at Zac. Oh, heavens, why didn't I think of all this before? she agonised silently.

Mary was still speaking as she led the way upstairs. 'We brought all Mr Wilding's things over from the stable flat and his clothes are in the dressing-room—we were sure that was what you'd want. And there's plenty of room for your clothes in your grandmother's big wardrobe.'

At last Mary left them alone and Kathryn turned and looked at Zac. She saw that he was grinning at her. 'I don't know why you look so shocked,' he said calmly. 'You might have guessed that this was what they'd do.'

She didn't answer immediately but stood staring at the big bed which seemed to dominate the room. Then she looked up at him again. 'Well?' she asked, 'what do we do now?'

For answer, he walked across the room and opened the door to the dressing-room and looked in. Then he turned back to her and she saw that the grin had disappeared. 'Don't worry, I won't bother you,' he said. 'There's a divan in the dressing-room. I'll sleep there.'

'Oh.' She paused for a moment, then added: 'But what will the servants think?'

'My dear girl, does it matter what they think?' His voice was cool and distant and he was already leaving the room. 'Surely that's our business.'

CHAPTER EIGHT

OVER the next few weeks they settled down to their new life together, which in so many ways was exactly as it had been before yet at the same time in so many ways so different. Zac immediately immersed himself in estate business and was often away from the house and the office all day. Kathryn told herself that this was obviously necessary if he were to carry out his duties conscientiously and efficiently, but a little voice inside her would insist on being heard, and what that voice said was that he had never kept out of her way to such an extent before they were married. Often he was out for the best part of two or three days at a time, only returning late in the evening for dinner, which they now took together in the huge dining-room. At least this was some improvement, Kathryn admitted grudgingly, remembering how she had hated dining alone in the weeks and months after Gran's death.

They also breakfasted together, but this was a largely silent meal, Zac burying himself behind the paper and Kathryn absorbed in her private thoughts, reading the few letters she received and wondering with increasing curiosity who could be the sender of the letters which had begun regularly to arrive for Zac, always addressed in the same rather flamboyant handwriting, sometimes as many as two in the same week, which he always picked up without comment and put in his pocket.

Kathryn was convinced that they were from a woman, almost certainly from someone whom he had left behind in Ireland and whose existence she had suspected for a long time, but she knew she couldn't ask him to enlighten her and tried to ignore the constant stream of letters and to pretend she didn't care.

With Zac away so much she became irritable and touchy, so that when they did meet in the evening she was often on edge and poor company. Usually when she snapped at him he would look at her in silence for a while, then continue with whatever he had been doing before she interrupted, but one evening, when as she knew full well she was being particularly tiresome and unreasonable, he slammed shut the book he was reading and stood up. 'What the devil is the matter with you lately?' he asked impatiently. 'You do nothing but moan and whine. I put in a hell of a long day running this place—without much help from you, I might add—and I don't mind telling you I'm dog tired and if you're trying to pick a fight I have no intention of giving you the satisfaction of rising to the bait. Now, suppose you tell me what this is all about once and for all, then perhaps I can get some peace and quiet. What's the matter, aren't you happy?'

Surprised by the unexpectedness of his response to her goading, she looked back at him for a moment without speaking, then she found her voice, and when she did her tone was sarcastic and biting. 'Of course I'm wildly happy. Who wouldn't be when they're left alone all day with no one to talk to and nothing to do!'

'Nothing to do!' Zac replied disgustedly. 'Don't

be absurd! You must be bone idle to say that! There must be a hundred things you could do. Don't be so bloody childish!'

'I suppose you're right up to a point,' she bit back, 'if I wanted to make silly little jobs for myself—just to keep me occupied and out of mischief—but that's not what I want and you know damn well it isn't! It wasn't like this before we were married, you know it wasn't. We did things together, discussed them and made decisions together, but now you seem to have shut me out completely and you're almost never here during the day at all. I must say, I think this is one hell of a marriage!'

At her last words, she clearly saw the anger drain out of him. 'Oh, so that's what this is all about, is it? I did wonder once or twice, but it seemed ridiculous and I decided I must be wrong.' He looked down at her and when she looked briefly up at him she saw that his expression was a mixture of pity and impatience and she suddenly wished that she had not goaded him into a confrontation. 'My dear girl,' he said after a moment's strained silence, 'Aren't you rather missing the point?'

At that, her head came up again and she frowned back at him. 'I don't understand.'

'Obviously.' His voice was suddenly full of contempt. 'You silly little idiot, have you forgotten what this so-called marriage is all about? We went into it for one reason and one reason only, and that was to save Woollerson. Nothing more. No strings. No love.' The way he spat out the word 'love' made her feel cold and sick inside, but there was another reason for the wave of paralysing bitterness that swept over her, and that was the realisation that she could have saved them both from the meaningless and arid emptiness of their relationship if she had only had the honesty to tell him about the letter which had made the whole venture unnecessary. She knew that she would feel a deep sense of guilt for the rest of her life, and she listened to him dully when she realised that he was still speaking. 'This is not and never can be a real marriage,' he said stonily. 'And you've known that—as I have—from the start. You disappoint me, Kathryn. I thought we understood one another and were going to make a success of it. Remember, it was your idea in the first place, and we agreed—if not in so many words—that saving Woollerson was worth the sacrifice of our personal wishes and feelings. It suited us both and I thought we could make it work. It seems I was wrong.' She really had no words that would seem in any way appropriate at that moment, so she said nothing, but she was totally unprepared for Zac's next words. 'Of course,' he said in a suddenly jeering and deliberately offensive tone, 'if you're looking for a stallion, you'd better find a stud farm. Sex between us is out of the question.'

It was just as well that he left the room then, because Kathryn was so devastated and revolted by the coarseness and vulgarity of his remark that anger and disgust boiled violently up inside her, and she leapt to her feet and a stream of abuse issued from her lips and hurled themselves impotently at the closed door. Words that a nicely brought up young girl would normally have denied even knowing hung on the air, turning it blue enough to bring a blush to the faces of her respectable ancestors in their portraits on the walls, and she stamped her foot in frustration because she was denied the satisfaction of saying them to his face. And it didn't help at all that she knew perfectly well that his disgusting words were by no means one hundred per cent wide of the mark.

That night she slept badly, tossing and turning for hours until finally falling into an exhausted sleep full of unpleasant dreams, dreadful forebodings and a black pall of misery hanging over everything. She woke some time in the early hours and groaned aloud when she saw that it was not yet daylight. The big bed felt hot and uncomfortable, and she got up and straightened the sheets, then went over to the window and stood looking out into the night. Then she turned her head, startled by the sound of a door opening, and saw Zac standing in the doorway of the dressing-room.

'What's the matter?' he asked sleepily. 'Can't you sleep?'

'No. I'm sorry if I disturbed you. Go back to bed.' Kathryn spoke stiffly, not having exchanged a word with him since their horrible conversation after dinner, and she was surprised that he did not immediately do as she suggested.

Instead he crossed the room until he was standing beside her, then took her by the hand and led her back to the bed. 'I'll see you settled first,' he said quietly. 'It's the least I can do, since I imagine I'm at least partly responsible for your not being able to sleep. I apologise for what I said. It was unforgivable.'

'I'm all right. It doesn't matter,' Kathryn said

dully, climbing into bed and allowing him to pull the covers over her. 'Perhaps we could start again. I'm sorry I've been such a pain. I'll find something to do.'

'Yes.' His tone was noncommittal but not unfriendly. 'You get some sleep now and we'll talk in the morning.'

'Zac——' On impulse she stopped him in the act of returning to his own bed. 'Can I ask you something?' He only grunted in reply, but she decided to finish what she'd begun, thinking that perhaps his answer might provide an explanation for the existence of the very apparent vacuum between them. 'Why did you say you were not the marrying kind?'

'Did I say that?' She couldn't see his expression in the dark and his voice gave nothing away.

'Yes, that night when I came over to the flat and told you about Gran's will. You turned me down then. Remember?'

'Oh, yes, so I did. I don't really think we want to go into that now.'

'You're in love with someone you left behind in Ireland, aren't you?' At last she had said it, and although she could feel his antagonism, she was glad the words were out in the open, but there was such a long silence that she was afraid that he wasn't going to answer her at all and that the next sound she would hear would be that of the dressing room door closing behind him. But she was wrong, and his answer came eventually.

'Your feminine intuition has been working overtime, I see,' he said heavily. 'You're right up a point—it was my reason for leaving Ireland.'

'What happened? Why did you have to leave?' And why did you have to come here of all places? she added silently.

'If you must know, she married my brother. Satisfied?' His voice was suddenly vicious, and Kathryn gasped at what she guessed to be the pain behind his words, shocked to her very bones by his bitter revelation.

'Oh, Zac, I'm sorry I asked! I never imagined . . .'

'Little girls shouldn't pry, should they?' he said harshly. 'Now get some sleep.' He walked over to the dressing room door, then paused with his hand on the door handle. 'And don't please waste any pity on me, will you? It's all over and done with. Forgotten. Goodnight.'

Although the atmosphere between them had improved a little, the next few weeks saw very little change in Kathryn's day-to-day existence, and now that she knew that Zac was in love with his brother's wife, she gave up all hope of altering their relationship or realising her earlier ambition of eventually sharing a normal married life with him. True, he did appear to make an effort to spend a little more time with her in the office, but she still spent the greater part of her day alone, and one afternoon, when he had gone off to visit an outlying farm without issuing an invitation to her to accompany him, in search of distraction and more or less on impulse she telephoned the riding stables and booked herself a ride. After all, she told herself as she got ready, there was no need for her to see Brian, and if she did there need be no embarrassment between them. He meant nothing to her now. All she wanted was a quiet ride alone, and she really couldn't see any reason why she shouldn't have just that.

All the same she was glad that there was no sign of Brian when she arrived at the stables, and soon she was walking her mount down the lane towards open country, relieved to be doing something positive at last and enjoying the feel of a horse beneath her again after so long. There was a sharp nip in the autumn air which brought colour to her cheeks and a sparkle to her eyes. She felt more cheerful than she had for weeks as she eased her mount into a canter, and although clouds were gathering to the west she judged that the threatened rain would hold off long enough for her to have her ride without getting a soaking. Although the horse was new to her he seemed amenable enough, and she soon allowed her concentration to relax and let him choose where they should go. This was fun, this was great, it was suddenly good to be alive!

Seeing a gate ahead, she took command again and set the powerful animal under her in line to jump, and the wind whistled past her as they thundered across the springy turf to within a few feet of the gate, when the horse suddenly swerved to one side so sharply that she was thrown clean over the gate and crashed down on to the hard ground beyond with one leg twisted awkwardly beneath her and her head spinning round drunkenly from where it had somehow managed to hit the top of the gate. For a moment she lay where she was, hoping that the giddiness would pass. Then she carefully got to her feet, only to collapse on to the ground once more as an agonising pain shot through her right knee. 'Damn it!' She swore aloud, disgusted with the horse, herself and fate for spoiling what had been developing into the best idea she'd had in ages. Also her head was still swimming crazily, and with a groan she lay down, hoping that a short rest would put things right.

When she sat up again a few minutes later, she looked round dazedly for the horse, but there was no sign of him and she was glad, because sooner or later he would almost certainly find his way back to the stables and thereby raise the alarm. By now she had admitted that she was going to need help to get home. Her knee was swelling up and hurting her badly and the slightest movement brought a renewal of the excruciating pain, and the way her head was still revolving crazily was making her feel sick. So she lay down and waited for someone to come and find her. At first she didn't mind too much because lying down was a great deal more comfortable than sitting up, but when the rain started to fall it was a different matter. This was no light shower, but a steady downpour, and she was soon soaked to the skin and becoming very cold. To add to her miseries, darkness was falling, and for the first time she acknowledged a growing anxiety that a search party would not be able to find her in the dark. The obvious thing to do was to start shouting, which she proceeded to do every few minutes, but it still felt as if she had been lying there for hours before she thankfully heard voices in the distance, accompanied by the unmistakable sound of a dog barking, and it was Bess who reached her first, bounding joyfully up to her and covering her face with wet kisses, then darting off again excitedly to tell the others that her beloved mistress had been found.

As it happened, Zac and Brian reached her more or less at the same moment, and she was momentarily blinded by the light of the torches which they had brought with them. She felt strong arms lift her and gratefully rested her aching head against the rough tweed jacket, but it wasn't until he spoke that she knew to whom it belonged. 'Move out of the way, man,' he said tersely. 'I'll take care of my wife. You lead the way with your torch.'

Half an hour later they were home, and Zac carried her up to their bedroom, where he sat her down on the edge of the bed and quickly stripped off her soaking wet clothes. Half swooning from the pain brought on by the removal of the boot from her injured leg, Kathryn uttered not one word of protest as she sat for a few moments completely naked while Zac went through to the bathroom to fetch a towel. Without a word he rubbed her briskly all over, then threw the towel on the floor as he gently slipped her nightdress over her head, then lifted her up and into the bed, pulling the covers up to her chin as Mary appeared in the doorway with hot water bottles. 'I've sent for the doctor,' he said as he and Mary put the hot water bottles on either side of her, 'just to be on the safe side, although it probably isn't necessary.'

Kathryn vaguely remembered thanking him, but knew nothing more until she opened her eyes to find the doctor bending over her. 'As your husband rightly diagnosed,' he said after he had examined her, 'you have a mild concussion and a badly twisted knee. Nothing too serious, I'm glad to say. I'll leave some pills to make sure you get a good night's rest and I'll strap up the knee. Keep off it for a day or two.' When he had dealt with her knee and was in the act of leaving, he paused with his hand on the doorknob. 'You're far too thin, Kathryn,' he said. 'Is anything the matter?'

'No, of course not,' she replied weakly, then closed her eyes and hoped he would go.

'Humph,' she heard him say, then: 'Time you started a family, my girl. That'll put you right.' And he had gone before she recovered sufficiently to say very quietly: 'I'm afraid that's quite out of the question.' Then Zac came back into the room and, making a conscious effort to focus her eyes on him, Kathryn thought he looked unusually pale. 'I'm sorry to have been such a idiot,' she muttered awkwardly. 'Thanks for being so kind.' Then she blinked rapidly once or twice, taken aback by the anger she detected in his voice.

'Kind? What an extraordinary word to use! What the hell did you expect? I'm not a monster, you know.' Before she could think of anything to say he had walked out of the room, and she frowned as she tried to collect her thoughts and fathom out the reason for his sudden explosion. But she found it quite impossible to clear her head and soon drifted into sleep, a deep sleep which lasted right through the night.

A few days later when she was sitting in the drawing-room reading, her leg stretched out in front of her on a footstool but feeling a great deal better, Zac came into the room, and stood looking down at her in silence for a few moments. Kathryn looked up enquiringly. It was almost lunchtime and it was a long time since they had lunched together, and she guessed that Zac had reverted to his habit of having a ploughman's lunch at the Red Lion, since he was never home in the middle of the day.

'Kathryn, I want a word with you,' he said abruptly. 'Do you think you're over your fall?'

'Yes, I'm fine,' she answered in surprise. 'My knee's still a bit stiff, that's all.' She was touched by his apparent concern but not prepared for his next words.

'In that case, I'd like to go away for a few days, maybe a week. Would you mind?'

'Of course not,' she replied evenly. Her emotions were well under control these days and she impatiently brushed aside a small pang at the realisation that he had not really been primarily concerned with her health. 'Where are you going?'

'Home—Ireland, that is. There's some unfinished business I must see to. Sure you'll be all right?'

It needed all her self-control to hide from him the dismay which his words had caused her. She was upset to know that he still thought of Ireland as his home, but this feeling was as nothing compared with the frank horror that seized her at the thought of losing him completely, convinced as she was that he had suddenly found he could not stay away from his brother's wife any longer. But somehow she found her voice and managed to say quite casually: 'Of course. When did you think of going?'

'Tomorrow, if that's all right with you. I'll be staying with the Reillys if you need me.'

When he had left the room, Kathryn sat very still, determinedly fighting down her rising panic, vividly recalling the steady stream of letters from Ireland, always in the same hated handwriting, never referred to by either of them. Also she was hurt by the realisation that the Reillys whom she had liked so much might be helping him to untangle himself from a marriage which they had appeared to favour. What she had been dreading for some time appeared to be happening, and she told herself that it served her right for deceiving him about the letter and virtually trapping him into marrying her. Dishonesty hardly ever paid, and she should have known better. In any case, it would be pointless to tell him now; it was much too late for that.

After he had gone and with the thought never far from her mind that he might never come back, Kathryn spent long hours in the office, partly for something to do to keep her mind off Zac and partly in the grim determination to get on with the job and show everyone that she could manage without him if she had to. But he had left everything in perfect order and there was little real work for her to do, and after a day or so she tired of sitting staring at the wall. Her knee was almost back to normal and she decided that it was time she rode again if she wasn't to risk losing her nerve.

When she arrived at the stables the first person she ran into was Brian, and when he insisted on accompanying her when she rode out she made only a token protest, really not caring one way or the other. Her heart had been cold and frozen inside her for a long time now and there was only one person who could warm her and bring her back to life, and that most emphatically was not Brian. As they rode quietly side by side in the cold December air she wondered idly what on earth she had ever seen in him. His mouth was weak, she could see that now, and he had an extremely irritating laugh which soon began to get on her nerves. She also found his conversation boring and only listened to him with half her attention, until something he said brought a sharp frown to her brow when she realised that he was trying to chat her up. She was incredulous and appalled to think that he could have the colossal nerve to think she would for one moment be interested in him when she was married to a man like Zac. Then she suddenly saw the funny side of it and decided to ignore his clumsy efforts at gallantry and try to enjoy the ride. Fortunately he took the hint and desisted, but when Kathryn decided that she would like to ride again the following day, he took up where he had left off and this time went further, attempting to kiss her when they had dismounted to give the horses a breather. Angrily, she had pushed him away and hurriedly remounted and cantered swiftly back to the stables, bitterly reflecting that this relief from her worries was now denied her.

Zac had been away for a week when he suddenly reappeared, bursting into the office where she was sitting idly scanning the accounts. He slammed the door to behind him and leant heavily against it while he glared down at her. The expression on his face extinguished the joy that had leapt inside her at the sight of him and the words of welcome on her lips were never uttered. 'What the hell have you been up to while I've been away?' he demanded without preamble. 'There's gossip about you all over the village!'

'What on earth are you talking about?' She glared back at him, then caught the smell of drink on his breath. 'You're drunk!'

'Don't think you can get out of it by attacking me, dear wife,' he snapped disgustedly. His blue eyes flashed and there was angry colour in his cheeks. 'There's no point in denying it—you were seen. With your effete boy-friend from the stables, as you very well know!'

'What you're saying,' she said, keeping her voice calm with the greatest difficulty, 'is that I was seen out riding with Brian, isn't it? Well, what's wrong in that, for God's sake? What possible harm could that do?'

'It was more than that and you know it,' said Zac, his voice suddenly weary. 'But if you really want me to spell it out I will. You were seen kissing that oaf. I heard it in the Red Lion not ten minutes ago.' Suddenly he came over to the desk and yanked her roughly round to face him, then bent swiftly and kissed her brutally, punishingly hard on the lips, knocking her head back against the wall as he did so. 'That's just to remind you that you're my wife and to emphasise the fact that you will kindly see to it that you are not available to that lout ever again!' Then he abruptly turned his back on her and walked to the door, but before he opened it he spoke again. 'This was hardly the homecoming I'd envisaged. I think it might be better if I moved back into the flat for the time being. We can't go on like this.'

CHAPTER NINE

ONCE he had moved back into the flat over the stables, Kathryn saw virtually nothing of Zac. The whole household was visibly affected by the obvious split between them and there was an almost tangible atmosphere of tension hanging over Woollerson, as if everyone was holding their breath, waiting either for a reconciliation or a complete break. Kathryn herself was torn between a longing to run away and put the greatest possible distance between them so that she would be out of range of his barbed tongue, should he decide to resume some sort of contact with her, and a weakness which kept her from doing anything positive, a weakness engendered by the love and respect she still felt for him in spite of everything. Her recent contact with Brian had shown her very clearly that Zac was worth ten of him, and although she told herself over and over again that she was being naïve and totally unrealistic in entertaining any such thoughts, she still hoped there was some sort of future for them. She wanted desperately to ask Zac about the outcome of his trip to Ireland, but he never gave her the chance and she couldn't decide what significance if any she could put on the fact that he had come back at all.

To make matters infinitely worse, Christmas was almost upon them, and for the first time in her life she longed for the festival to be over. Last year

Gran had still been alive and there had been the usual traditional Christmas, the old hall decorated with holly and mistletoe, presents under the tree, turkeys, Christmas pudding and mince pies, and the yearly event of the party for the children from the village. This year Kathryn had done nothing whatever about a party, but she thought dully that probably no one would be expecting one, since she knew perfectly well that news of the split between her and Zac would have gone round the village like wildfire. However, at the last minute, she did drive into Haversham and buy Zac a present, thinking that she could hide it away and only give it to him in the extremely unlikely event of him having bought something for her.

Right up until the morning of Christmas Day itself, she had no idea whether he intended to join her for dinner. She didn't even know for certain whether he was actually even in the flat. He might well have gone away. In any case, there was no holly in the house this year, no tree shining in its accustomed corner of the drawing room, no air of jollity or festivity at all, and she had given no instructions to Cook one way or the other. Christmas dinner on her own would be no joke, but if that was what almost certainly was going to be the case, then she would just have to grit her teeth and get through it somehow. In the past she and Gran had had a light lunch and the children's party had started at three o'clock, with dinner at eight, and since she had not thought of giving the staff the time off until it was too late, she told Cook that dinner would be at the usual time and that, since she was not sure of Mr Wilding's plans, she should prepare enough for him as well in case he should join her at the last minute. She felt sure that Cook felt as awkward as she did herself when she was giving her orders, and she cursed herself for being too much of a coward to go over to the flat and ask Zac point blank. Eventually she sent Mary across with a note and was vaguely surprised at her own lack of emotion when she returned with the messsge that Zac would be glad to dine with her that night. Having held such ridiculously high hopes in the past, perhaps she was learning at last to expect nothing; that way at least she would not get hurt.

But she still could not entirely crush the small spurt of pleasure she experienced when he walked into the drawing-room just before eight o'clock, darkly handsome in his well-cut dinner jacket, a faint smile lighting up his hard lean face. She saw at once that he had a present for her, and he wished her a Happy Christmas as he handed her the gift-wrapped parcel.

'I've got something for you too,' she said, quickly undoing his present and finding an expensive-looking edition of the complete works of Jane Austen in dark red leather, tooled in gold.

'Thank you. It's beautiful.' A safe, impersonal kind of present, she realised, and she chided herself for ingratitude when she found herself thinking of the library stocked with books from floor to ceiling, among which undoubtedly was a set of the complete works of Jane Austen. Quickly she left the room and ran upstairs to fetch her present, which she too had had gift-wrapped in the shop in Haversham, then returning, she watched him in his turn take off the wrapping paper to reveal an equally expensive-looking, equally impersonal leather writing case.

Suddenly he grinned across at her and this time the smile reached his eyes. 'We were both playing safe, I see,' he said. 'It's very nice. Thank you.'

Dinner was a lot less awkward than Kathryn had expected, Zac making a noticeable effort to be entertaining. They drank a great deal of wine and the atmosphere between them mellowed considerably, and Kathryn realised with some surprise that she was quite definitely enjoying herself, until, after a long pause, Zac suddenly became serious. 'Kathryn, we have to talk,' he said quietly. 'And this seems to be as good a time as any.'

The smile was abruptly wiped off her face and the familiar coldness crept over her once more, deadening the feeling of warmth, almost of happiness, which had gradually enveloped her as the evening wore on. This is it, an inner voice told her, this is what you've been waiting for. She was so sure of what he was going to tell her and she was also so determined that he would never guess what his words would do to her that she quickly held up her hand to silence him. 'Please, Zac, don't say anything. Let me speak first.' She was proud of the calmness of her tone, the absolute steadiness of her voice. 'As you say, we might as well get it over and be civilised about it. It hasn't worked, has it? Wasn't that what you were going to say? I'm sure it was, and of course you're absolutely right. No, please, don't interrupt. Let me be the one to say it. Do you want a divorce? Or I suppose it would be an annulment under the circumstances.' She managed to keep all traces of bitterness out of her words and she found that giving voice to thoughts which had been plaguing her and giving her very little peace for many weeks brought its own bitter-sweet relief. But she kept her head bent over her plate during the long silence which ensued, afraid that she might waver if she were to meet his eyes.

At last he spoke, and to her ears his voice sounded thin and tight and she was grateful to him for making it plain that he was not wholly unaffected by what she had at last managed to put into words and bring into the open. 'If that's what you want, Kathryn.'

'Be honest—it's what we both want, Zac,' she said, her voice almost faltering. 'And the sooner the better.'

She heard him get up from his chair and quickly stole a glance at his face. He looked unusually pale, she noticed, but that was understandable. Presumably he had feelings the same as anyone else and no one could expect to enjoy what they were going through. 'Would you like me to see Mr Barnes for you?' he asked. 'I imagine he would be the right person to sort out this mess.' He allowed a hint of bitterness to creep into his last sentence, but she refused to be drawn.

'Thanks, I'd be grateful if you would.' She looked away from him quickly then and she was sickeningly glad when she heard the dining-room door close behind him. For a few moments she sat where she was, struggling valiantly to hold on to her self-control, fighting a losing battle against the wave of misery which was rapidly overtaking her, until she was powerless to resist any longer, when she buried her face in her hands and gave way to a torrent of bitter scalding tears that racked her entire body.

As was customary, on Boxing Day the staff had the whole day off and Kathryn had the house to herself. There was no sign of Zac, for which she was thankful, knowing that she could not hope to hide her misery from him should they chance to meet so soon after their conversation of the night before. In fact she hoped she need never see him again as long as she lived, although common sense told her that this hope was unlikely to be fulfilled. There would presumably be formalities to be gone through which would require the presence of them both in the painful business of untying the bond so recently made between them, but she hoped most fervently that Mr Barnes would spare her as much as he could. She knew she would have to talk to him sooner or later, but was grateful to Zac for offering to make the first move.

On the following day she felt calmer and more able to accept the fact that everything was over between them, but once she had, she was seized by an overwhelming desire to get away from Woollerson, if only for a few days. There was still no sign of Zac and the house was very quiet, the staff behaving almost as if there had been another death in the family, until Kathryn felt she wanted to scream. It might be cowardly to run away, but she really didn't care, and in any case, from now on her actions were entirely her affair and of no concern to anyone but herself. In this defiant mood she quickly packed a bag and told Cook that she was going away for a few days, carefully avoiding the older woman's eyes as she did so, knowing full well what she would see if she looked at her directly. She carried her case over to the stables and threw it into the back of her car, making no effort to be quiet in case Zac was there, because she doubted very much if he would try to stop her; there was no earthly reason why he should.

As she got into the gleaming little sports car she wondered whether she would be able to keep it, or whether her conscience would force her to give it back to Zac. Then she shook her head impatiently and set her mouth in a firm straight line, determined not to think about Zac or their disastrous marriage. She had not decided to get away in order to spend the time wallowing in misery and regret and vain longings for a future which had been a non-starter from the beginning. She just wanted a break and to get away from the atmosphere of tension which pervaded Woollerson, that was all. She drove round to the house to collect Bess whom she had decided to take with her for company, then without a backward glance set off quickly down the drive.

When, several hours later, she drove down the narrow main street of the little port of Blakeney, she wondered whether she had known all along that she would come back here. It had not been a conscious decision to return, of that she was certain. It was almost as if the car had driven itself back to where she and Zac had experienced some good times—if not very many—and where she had briefly allowed herself to entertain hopes of a good future with him. Once again she quickly shook her head to rid it of thoughts which were straying on to dangerous ground, and drew up outside the post office where she decided to make enquiries about renting a cottage for a few days. She knew she couldn't go back to the hotel and was well pleased with what she found when, half an hour later, she let herself into the end cottage of the row which she and Zac had discovered on their honeymoon. It was fully equipped down to the last detail and although the rate was high for an out-of-season letting, it was inclusive of electricity and central heating, and Kathryn took it for a week, with an option to extend if she wished. It was, she decided, a delightfully snug bolthole and would suit her very well.

She spent the afternoon buying groceries and tins of dog food, then, with Bess dancing clumsily and happily round her feet, set off for a long tramp across the marshes. In jeans and duffle coat and with a thick wool scarf of Zac's she had found in the hall at Woollerson wound round her neck, she was well protected against the cold, and she positively enjoyed the sting of the salt in the air which the wind threw in her face. The strong Norfolk air soon brought colour to her cheeks and blew away the cobwebs, and as she strode along she knew she was glad she had come.

It was almost dark when she and Bess returned to the cottage. It was also appreciably colder, and she was grateful for the blast of warm air which met them when she turned the key in the lock and went inside. When she had turned on the lights and the curtains were drawn, she went through to the little white-painted kitchen and opened a tin of food for Bess, who was making it very clear that she was ravenously hungry, then realising that she herself was in much the same condition and suddenly remembering that she had omitted to have any lunch, Kathryn buttered herself thick slices of fresh new bread while the kettle was boiling, then took the wrapping off a rich fruit cake and, when the tea was made, put everything on a tray and carried it through to the sitting-room. Then she sank down into a deep chintz-covered armchair and hungrily attacked the fragrant locally-baked bread. It was very good and she ate it all, as well as two large slices of cake, accompanied by several cups of hot strong tea then, her hunger satisfied and with a very contented Bess lying across her feet, she snuggled down into the softness of the armchair and fell asleep.

It was on the evening of her third day in Blakeney that she was woken by a loud hammering on the door. It was barely ten o'clock, but she had gone to bed early because another day tramping with Bess across the salt marshes had made it quite impossible to keep awake until her normal bedtime, and the moment her head hit the pillow she had been asleep. The knocking persisted, accompanied by loud barking from Bess, and although she was a little wary about answering the door, Kathryn switched on the light and got out of bed. Then she went down to the foot of the stairs, shrugging into her dressing-gown as she went. 'Idiot!' she said to Bess, whose tail she saw was wagging furiously. 'You're supposed to protect me, not act as a welcoming committee!' Then she called out to whoever was standing on the other side of the door, 'Who is it?' The answer she received made her gasp with surprise, but she unbolted the door and stood aside as Zac strode into the tiny hall and closed the door behind him. 'What on earth are you doing here?' she asked. ''and how did you know where I was?'

'Intuition. It took a little time,' was all the reply she got. Then he turned round and his eyes looked over her shoulder. 'So that's where my scarf got to. I thought I'd left it at one of the farms.'

'You surely didn't come all this way to find your scarf!' she exploded, suddenly very angry with him for invading her privacy and undoing all the good the past few days had done her. 'Perhaps you'd tell me why you're here and then go. I was asleep.'

'So I perceive. You look delightfully flushed and rumpled.' Kathryn frowned, trying unsuccessfully to gauge his mood. He was looking at her with a very odd expression indeed on his face and, at his remark, she quickly put up a hand to smooth her hair, but his arm shot out and he gripped her wrist. 'Don't do that,' he said quietly. 'You'll quite spoil the effect.'

'Zac! Stop fooling and tell me why you're here.' She was determined to keep her cool and not let him get past the protective barrier she had carefully been erecting over the past few days between herself and any further hurt, but he was making it extremely difficult for her.

'I saw old Barnes today,' he said softly, looking down at her where she was still imprisoned close to him by his continued grip on her wrist.

'You surely didn't come all this way to tell me that either,' she said dully.

'Oh, but I did.' His voice held an obvious hidden meaning and she looked up into his face with eyes narrowed. 'And guess what he told me.' Her knees suddenly turned to jelly and the colour drained from her face as she realised without any doubt at all what he was driving at. Zac laughed softly. 'Poor old boy, he didn't mean to betray a client's confidence and he was most upset when he realised that you'd never told me. Look at me, Kathryn. You know what I'm talking about, don't you?' Quite unable to speak, she nodded but wouldn't look at him, until his free hand tilted her chin up and she was forced to look into the brilliant blue eyes burning down at her. 'Why didn't you tell me about the letter? I'm afraid I really must insist on an answer, wife of mine. It's very important.' He sighed as she remained silent, the colour coming and going in her face as she struggled to think of an explanation which he would accept to excuse her conduct. Then he let go of her wrist and seized her shoulders and shook her impatiently. 'Can't you see how important it is, you little idiot!' he suddenly shouted at her. 'You must answer! Why didn't you tell me?'

Suddenly her head came up and she glared angrily back at him. 'Stop it, you damned bully! All right, I'll tell you, if you must know, then perhaps you'll go. I didn't tell you because, fool that I was, I found that I actually wanted to marry you!' She laughed bitterly. 'I thought we could really make a go of it and that it suited both of us. I know it was dishonest and wrong of me and I did try to tell you, truly I did, but ... well, I didn't. I'm sorry, I know I behaved badly, but remember, at that time I didn't know about your brother's wife. I thought you were free, as free as I was. I would have told you if I'd known you were in love with someone else.' She stopped speaking, but he remained silent, not helping her at all. He still had both hands on her shoulders and when she tried to wriggle out of his grasp the pressure of his hands tightened. 'What are you going to do now, Zac?' she asked at last when the silence had gone on for as long as she could stand it. 'Are you going to live with her?'

'I have the distinct impression,' he said, speaking slowly and deliberately and completely ignoring her question, 'that you're not telling the whole truth. I've come to know you pretty well, Kathryn, and I think I can tell when you're hiding something. What is it? I have to know.' They continued to stare at one another and when it was obvious that she had no intention of answering him, he sighed deeply, then said very quietly: 'It couldn't possibly be that you love me, could it, Kathryn?'

The words hung in the air between them as she felt his hands slip round to the back of her neck and begin to stroke the softness of her bare flesh, then run up into her hair until, with a cry, she wrenched herself out of his grasp and ran towards the stairs. 'Yes, it could!' She almost spat the words at him as she climbed the first few steps on legs which were shaking uncontrollably. '*Now* are you satisfied, you swine!' She wanted to get away from him as quickly as possible, but her legs were strangely slow in responding and she choked back a sob as she heard him bound across the room and drag her back down the stairs and into his arms.

'At last!' She heard the triumph in his voice as

she lay against him, helplessly trapped by the strength of his arms about her. 'Why did you have to make it so difficult for me, you stubborn little darling! Oh God, if I'd only known!' Then his hard mouth found hers and, utterly bewildered, she made not the slightest attempt to resist. She felt as if she were drowning and when, half fainting, she imagined dimly that she was going down for the third and final time, Zac scooped her up into his arms and carried her up the stairs and into the bedroom, depositing her gently on the bed and kneeling on the floor beside her. 'Tell me again!' he said urgently, tugging at the cord of her dressing-gown. 'Tell me you love me!'

'Zac, I don't understand,' she whispered, beginning to tremble as the dressing-gown fell from her shoulders and he pushed her down until she was lying full length on the bed.

'Never mind about that,' he said impatiently. 'Just say it!'

'I love you,' she said simply, wide eyes searching his face, hardly daring to believe what she thought she saw in his eyes.

'And I love you, my dearest, dearest wife, and have done almost since the moment I first set eyes on you,' he said, while he pushed down the shoulder straps of her nightdress with hands which were not quite steady. 'Oh, what fools we've been!'

'Zac, wait!' She put her hands over his. 'I must know. What about your brother's wife? Don't you love her?'

'That was over a long time ago. I soon realised that she was a rather cheap little gold-digger who thought she could have her cake and eat it.'

'But all those letters that kept arriving—they were from her, weren't they? Oh, how I hated that!'

'That's why I had to go over to Ireland. I had to make her realise that it was finished between us and that I had a very beautiful wife in England whom I loved very much indeed.'

'I was so glad to see you when you came home. I thought perhaps you weren't coming back. But then you were so angry. Was that because you were jealous? I never imagined . . .'

'You bet I was!' His hands moved impatiently under hers, but she still gripped them tightly. 'How did you expect me to feel when I heard the gossip about you and that clot of a boy-friend of yours! As a matter of fact I went over to the riding stables and punched him on the nose. I enjoyed that.' A grim smile briefly lit up his face, and Kathryn felt an extraordinary sensation of warmth begin to steal over her.

'*Ex*-boy-friend, Zac,' she murmured, gazing up at him. 'Poor Brian, I can't imagine what I ever saw in him.' Then the smile faded from her face as she remembered. 'But why did you move back into the flat? I thought it was to show me that it was all over between us.'

'I thought it would give us a breathing space and a chance to start again. It seemed like a good idea at the time.' Zac broke her grip on his hands and began to run his hands over her body. 'Kathryn, for God's sake,' he groaned, 'don't make me wait any longer!' Then she reached up and wrapped her arms tightly round him, overwhelmed by the sudden joy of being able to show her love for him at last. She felt him pull her nightdress down until she was naked and his eyes were filled with a deep hunger as he looked down at her. 'We'll have a proper honeymoon right here,' he said in a voice which was infinitely tender, yet exultant and triumphant at the same time. Then he turned off the light, and in a few moments she felt the heat from the full length of his naked body beside her on the bed as, with his mouth on hers, he whispered: 'Starting now.'

Harlequin Plus

A WORD ABOUT THE AUTHOR

Two threads are woven through the tapestry of Helen Dalzell's life: storytelling and romance. She was born in Highgate, north London, and as a child was difficult and awkward—a trial to all but her doting father and any nanny who was better than average at telling bedtime tales.

When she was ten, Helen tried her hand at creating her own story (years later, she found the manuscript of it carefully kept by her mother). When she was eleven, Helen fell in love. This romance netted no kisses, but she did receive from her admirer a prophetic gift—her first fountain pen.

Being a sickly child, Helen missed a lot of school, but she still managed to excel in English composition—though not yet realizing the full extent of her talent. In fact, it was a real-life romance with a wonderful man, her husband-to-be, that launched her on her career as a novelist. She had already gained success in magazine writing, but it took the encouragement of her husband—a captain in the merchant service—to set her on her way toward writing a full-length book.

Now, with several novels behind her and more, one hopes, ahead, she says that her heart always rules her head and that writing love stories for women is most appropriate for someone with her romantic past.

HARLEQUIN CLASSIC LIBRARY

Great old romance classics from our
early publishing lists.

FREE BONUS BOOK

On the following page is a coupon with
which you may order any or all of these titles.
If you order all nine, you will receive a FREE
book—*District Nurse,* a heartwarming classic
romance by Lucy Agnes Hancock.

The fourteenth set
of nine novels in the

HARLEQUIN CLASSIC LIBRARY

118 Then Come Kiss Me Mary Burchell
119 Towards the Dawn Jane Arbor
120 Homeward the Heart Elizabeth Hoy
121 Mayenga Farm Kathryn Blair
122 Charity Child Sara Seale
123 Moon at the Full Susan Barrie
124 Hope for Tomorrow Anne Weale
125 Desert Doorway Pamela Kent
126 Whisper of Doubt Andrea Blake

Great old favorites...
Harlequin Classic Library

Complete and mail this coupon today!

Harlequin Reader Service

In U.S.A.
1440 South Priest Drive
Tempe, AZ 85281

In Canada
649 Ontario Street
Stratford, Ontario N5A 6W2

Please send me the following novels from the Harlequin Classic Library. I am
enclosing my check or money order for $1.50 for each novel ordered, plus 75¢
to cover postage and handling. If I order all nine titles at one time, I will receive
a FREE book, *District Nurse*, by Lucy Agnes Hancock.

☐ 118   ☐ 121   ☐ 124
☐ 119   ☐ 122   ☐ 125
☐ 120   ☐ 123   ☐ 126

Number of novels checked @ $1.50 each =	$_____
N.Y. and Ariz. residents add appropriate sales tax	$_____
Postage and handling	$____.75
TOTAL	$_____

I enclose _____
(Please send check or money order. We cannot be responsible for cash sent
through the mail.)
Prices subject to change without notice.

Name _____
(Please Print)

Address _____
(Apt. no.)

City _____

State/Prov. _____

Zip/Postal Code _____

Offer expires March 31, 1984   3095600000